all we know of LOVE

all we know of LOVE

NORA RALEIGH BASKIN

CANDLEWICK PRESS

This is a work of fiction. Names, characters, places,
and incidents are either products of the author's
imagination or, if real, are used fictitiously.

First paperback edition 2013

Library of Congress Catalog Card Number 2007022396

ISBN 978-0-7636-3623-4 (hardcover)
ISBN 978-0-7636-6650-7 (paperback)

12 13 14 15 16 17 BVG 10 9 8 7 6 5 4 3 2 1

Printed in Berryville, VA, U.S.A.

This book was typeset in Granjon.

Candlewick Press
99 Dover Street
Somerville, Massachusetts 02144

visit us at www.candlewick.com

For Lyn Sommer

The bus tires thump over the road, which sounds like a pencil tapping rhythmically, which sounds like a heart beating slowly, which reminds me of something I can't quite shut my brain to, but makes me tired all the same. I look in the scratched mirror above the tiny metal sink and I see my reflection.

It is blurry, as if I am looking at myself underwater.

I am nearly at the end of a twenty-four-hour journey in search of something that, after all this time, I didn't realize I was looking for. But I know now, I am riding as much away from something as I am toward it. These things, these comings and goings, this ending and beginning, must be connected, like the completion of a sentence. Like the answer to a riddle, or a dream, in which all the people are really you.

Because there is a need to hear one story and to tell another.

Chapter One

That Love is all there is,
Is all we know of Love.
—Emily Dickinson

My mother was telling me something just before she left for good, taking nothing with her (as far as we could tell). Leaving behind everything she had ever bought, everything she had ever wanted, everything she owned or had ever been given.

And everything she had made: a lopsided clay bowl with the image of a tiny painted pineapple from her ceramic workshop days, a collage of family pictures cut in various sizes and shapes, pasted together and framed. She spent weeks on that. All the pressed wildflowers she had collected and laminated between sheets of clear plastic to last forever. And me.

Me, she left behind.

She walked out mid-sentence, before she finished what she was about to say.

It was a long time ago already, four years. Four years, four months, and fifteen days to be exact. And for four years, four months, and *twelve* days, I didn't think for one second about what she never finished telling me. I gave no thought at all to her unfinished sentence. I suppose it is like being in a car accident. You don't think about something as trivial as the conversation you were having at the moment of impact. Not until weeks later, if at all. It comes to you in daydream one day as you are remembering the crash, that awful crumbling-metal noise, and if you begin to reconstruct the instant at all, it may not be for months, or in my case, years.

At first all I cared about was that she was gone. I wrote her letters. I made her Mother's Day gifts. When she had been gone sixteen months and seven days, I sewed her an orange dinosaur pillow in FACs class. I cried at night, and at sad TV shows, and, for some unknown reason, during first-aid filmstrips shown in gym class on rainy days. And then I stopped. Because all things need to come to an end. Good things and bad things.

But then just recently I started to remember and I began to reconstruct. And wonder: if only I had let her say what it was she was about to tell me, would everything have been different? Would I be in this situation?

My mother stopped mid-sentence. She was in mid-thought, about to tell me something.

She was talking about love.

At the Stamford bus station, there is a little newsstand with chips and candy and gum, stuff like that. *I should load up on snacks,* I am thinking. I don't have anything I am going to need, except money, and not that much of that. The ticket was a hundred and twenty-six dollars, one way. When I called a few days ago to get the schedule, I found out how expensive the trip would be, and how long it would take. Twenty-four hours on a bus. I can't imagine that. I'll need some stuff to eat and drink, I guess. I should have made myself something at home, a sandwich or two, but I didn't think of it.

It's early. Way early, especially for a Saturday morning. It's not even seven thirty. And this kid working behind the newsstand isn't paying attention; he's reading a book. I've been standing here for a while. Sometimes the world reminds me of how invisible I am.

My dad tells me it's because my voice is too quiet, even when I'm shouting. He says it's loud enough, but the timbre's too soft, as if it were at a different frequency, like there's something wrong with it and nobody hears me.

"Excuse me," I say again, a second time. The boy who works at this newsstand is at that age. Not young, not old, so I don't know how to address him, to get his attention. *Mister? Kid?*

Hey, you seems rude.

"Hello there," I try. "Sir?"

Sir?

How stupid is that?

He looks up and smiles, like I just made a joke, when joking is the furthest thing from my mind. He is annoying me already.

"What can I get you?" he says. He lowers his book. I see he is wearing an orange T-shirt so faded its softness is almost visible. He hikes his jeans up over his skinny hips as he steps up to the counter. I see he is wearing a rope necklace around his neck, with one white shell that sits right in that spot, that little dip in a boy's neck that always seems a little too intimate to be looking at.

"Um . . . I'm not sure," I say, looking over everything, which all looks really unhealthy and fairly sickening.

"Stuff for your trip?" he asks me.

"Yeah." I nod. *My trip.*

"Where are you going?"

And when he asks me that, I know I am going to lie even before I open my mouth. Like I am trying it on for size, testing out my abilities.

"North Dakota," I say.

"North Dakota, huh?" He smiles.

This guy is flirting with me, I think. I used to like this, but ever since Adam flirting has taken on a whole new meaning. In a way, it's like I know what it means now. I know what can happen, and I don't know what I want from it anymore.

"That's a pretty long trip," he says.

I want to smile back, but suddenly I feel a wave of nausea. Maybe from looking at the candy, or from this older man, who comes up beside me and reeks of cigarettes. Or maybe it's something else entirely that scares me even more.

"Forget it," I say quickly to the boy. "I don't want anything."

And I hurry away.

At least this is one of those big buses, the kind you get for really long, expensive school field trips. The kind with upholstered seats and little TV screens every few rows. But the screens are blank. So far the seat next to me is empty. I am doing a silent prayer that it stays this way all the way to Florida.

It is such a long trip to be sitting next to someone you don't know, maybe someone awful. Someone fat. Every time a passenger walks down the aisle and then passes me by, I think I am that much closer to sitting alone. I am resting my head on the window, making it as hard as possible for someone to catch my eye.

So far so good.

The bus hisses and lurches forward. When we hit the highway, the sun is fully risen and on its way to completing another cycle, another day.

I make it all the way to New York City this way. Port Authority Bus Terminal, the driver announces. We have a half an hour wait here. We sit in our tall seats as the bus idles. The smoke from the exhaust blows up and across my window like a miniature H-bomb. The bus shakes as it idles, but I am grateful for the heat. I suppose it must be cold out. It's February. It was freezing when I slipped out of my house this morning, but we are in an underground terminal system of some kind. As the bus looped its way from the outside world into this subterranean one, a long line of overhead fluorescent lines became the sky. The gray of concrete has never seemed so oppressive to me before, or so final.

Although I suppose if I wanted, I could still get off here.

I am not that far from home. I'm in New York.

Big deal. I feel my legs start to move before my brain tells them to. I am about to stand, maybe get off the bus. It's like a twitching in my muscles, separate from my thoughts but maybe with more common sense.

But now all of a sudden people start getting on the bus, and again I am doing my soundless please-let-me-sit-alone invocation. The chances seem slimmer. The bus is filling up quickly. Still, somehow I am sitting by myself when the driver finishes putting the luggage away underneath and heaves himself up the steps and into his seat. Then just as he pulls the doors shut, the last passenger shuffles down the aisle toward me. She is a big woman with two big bags in her hands. One is some kind of massive tapestry pocketbook and the other a clear plastic bag of knitting paraphernalia. There is a needle threatening to poke out the bottom of the plastic one. Her bags move before her as if they are individual people unto themselves, and all three stop directly at my seat.

I lift my head from the window for a second, not too much so it looks like I want to say hello or anything, just enough to see who she is.

She sits down next to me.

Her skin is the color of coffee beans before they are ground, and shiny like that. She's pretty fat, too. She has knee-high stockings on that pinch the skin just below her knees, which I see when she plops that plastic bag onto her lap, and it makes her floral-patterned housedress rise up a little. She has on sandals, and her toes are painted a bright fuchsia. The tan mesh of her stockings dulls the color, but I can still see it. Sin City Pink, I imagine. Or Mango Tango.

I plop my head against the seat back and close my eyes. The bus is beginning to move, so if I had any plans to jump off and not go through with this, it's too late now. This is when I notice that I have had my cell phone clutched in my hand since Stamford. It has nearly come alive with a power of its own, a life force beyond its battery and cell-tower capabilities. It is my connection, my constant accessibility, because Adam might call. Because any moment of any minute, he *could* call.

And if Adam should call—

If he should call—

If he should call, I will be right here to feel the phone vibrate even before it rings.

I hold the phone and rest my head against the window and keep my eyes closed so I don't have to talk to the lady next to me. She has that look, like someone who likes to care about other people for no reason at all.

I hate that.

* * *

If I think really hard, I am pretty sure I remember my mother was doing the dinner dishes that evening. Her soapy hands were dipping in and out of the water, soft white bubbles stuck on the backs of her skinny wrists. My mother always shut off the water while she was washing and turned it on again to rinse. She hated to waste. Hated to use things up that didn't have to be, like squirting out more liquid soap than needed or taking two napkins when one would do. She folded and reused paper bags and even plastic bags. She was always telling me not to flush the toilet every time. There was no need to waste water and electricity.

That's disgusting and I'd flush anyway. Every time.

She officially objected to wrapping paper. She flat out refused to buy it. I'd show up at elementary-school birthday parties with my gift packaged in either wrinkled recycled wrapping paper or, worse, the Sunday funnies from the newspaper.

She turned the lights off whenever she left a room. Only turned on what she needed, so in winter our house sat in quiet darkness, illuminated in only one or two small areas. She unplugged the toaster and the coffee machine because she read somewhere they can drain a measurable amount of electricity even when they are not in use.

And when she did the dishes, she'd fill the sink with water, washing each dish and letting it sit. Then she'd turn the tap back on and rinse, efficiently turning each plate or cup or bowl over in her hands, running it under the stream of water and setting it on the rack on the counter.

It's been over four years, and it is still her hands I remember best. Her long fingers, and the raised veins that wove across the backs of her hands in geometric shapes. To this day I always look at a woman's hands and see beauty in long bony fingers, blue-veined skin, and short clean nails. A woman's hands. My mother hated her hands. She said they looked old, while I thought my mother's hands were beautiful.

Yes, I remember now we were in the kitchen.

She was talking to me and I was eating my dessert. But I wasn't happy, was I? They were the wrong cookies. I was in the mood for something chocolaty. She had given me oatmeal-raisin cookies and a glass of milk.

She just started talking. "I think I had it all wrong, Natalie. You know, my mother just gave me the worst advice. . . . You know, Nana. But it stuck with me."

My mother was facing the sink, so my last memories of her are of her back and her hands and the sound of splashing water and her voice. Some part of me knew that she was very upset. I knew she was crying. But a bigger part of me didn't want to hear it or see it.

I wanted different cookies. Chocolate cookies.

So I was just waiting for a pause in her monologue, when I could ask her if I could open a new box of cookies. It was a risk, I knew. My mother didn't like to open a new box until the old one was finished. She didn't like having things that didn't get completely used up, that would go stale and thus be wasted.

But I wanted *chocolate* cookies. Wasn't it a waste to eat something you didn't really want? Isn't that a waste, too?

I didn't like the look of her shoulders hunched over the sink, shaking. The deliberate movement of her arms reaching over and placing dish after dish in the draining rack. She was still talking, her voice quivering.

"I don't ever want to give you that kind of advice. . . ."

But I wasn't listening anymore. Her words turned into some kind of gibberish, some other language I couldn't understand and so didn't have to listen to. A grown-up language I wasn't supposed to hear. The more desperate she became, the more I wanted those chocolate cookies. I knew there were some in the pantry. I had seen them. I was sure.

I was just waiting for my moment to ask.

"There's something I want to tell you, Natty. . . ."

I already had a whole convincing argument ready for why opening a new box of cookies would make sense, be ultimately less wasteful. Just imagine my genius.

But my mother went on. "I mean, Natalie, I want to tell you. I think you should understand this about—"

Our voices collided and hers was swallowed up like beach sand under the tide. "Mom?"

"—about love."

I stopped her cold. "I want chocolate cookies."

She turned from the sink and looked right at me. Her eyes were swollen, even redder than I was expecting. Her face was wet, and her nose and her chin. She reached out with her hands because they were soapy and she couldn't wipe her eyes. She held them out as if she didn't know what else to do with them.

"I mean, Mom? Can I open the chocolate cookies? I saw some in the pantry. I know the oatmeal cookies aren't finished . . . but can I?"

I began to list my really good reasons, but I didn't have to.

"Sure, sweetie," my mother said. Her voice was strange.

I remember she walked over to the table where I

was sitting and took the half-empty package of oatmeal-raisin cookies. Then she stepped right over to our new trash can with its flip top. When we bought it I thought it was really cool. My mom stepped on the foot lever.

My heart stopped beating.

I was flooded with the sense that I had done something wrong. Very wrong.

I watched as my mother dropped the entire package of cookies into the garbage. Then she took the chocolate cookies from the pantry and placed them before me.

"Do you have enough milk?" she asked calmly. Her tears had dried, but her face still looked blotchy and awful.

I nodded, wide-eyed and fearful.

And she left.

She took her coat from the peg by the door. She jangled her keys in her pocket, and she stepped out quietly into the night.

When I was in fifth grade, about ten or eleven years old, just about a year before my mother decided to jump ship, bail out, skip town and never come back again, I had a very specific idea about who I was going to fall in love with. It never occurred to me then that he might not fall in love with me in return.

Such a thing as an Adam was beyond my imagining.

Such a thing as the agony that love brings had never entered my mind. Before Adam, love was a happy ending, like an episode of *Full House.* Or the kind of book your grandmother gives you.

We even had a list, my friend Sarah and I. I mean, a real list. Written down. On paper.

We would add to it whenever we got together, whenever we had a sleepover. It was an official rule. You packed your toothbrush, your hairbrush, lip gloss, pajamas, your favorite stuffed animal, and the list. The list traveled back and forth between our houses that entire year.

"I've got a new one," Sarah told me. Her out-of-breath voice betrayed her excitement. This would be a good one.

We were already in our pajamas. Sarah's mother had dragged out a futon, two pillows, sheets, two huge comforters and let us sleep in the front room: the den, with the TV, the DVD player, and the computer. We had spent most of the night IM-ing and the rest of the night watching the movie we had rented. It was now dark and quiet; the rest of the household had long since gone to bed. That was another rule. Writing on the list must be the last thing we did before we went to sleep, when we were too tired to do anything else, so thoughts of our true love would be our last thoughts before sleep and therefore penetrate our dreams.

That way, they would one day come true.

"OK, I'm ready," I said. I had had the list at my house, and now I took it out of my backpack and carefully unfolded it. The paper was threatening to break apart at the folds. It hung limp and I had to support it from the underside on my open palm.

"Read," Sarah commanded.

I began. We had eleven written requirements for our true love so far. I would read each one, and then Sarah would present her latest. Then we would vote. If we both agreed, it would then be added to the list. So far only one suggestion had been voted off: He must be handsome.

We argued about this for a while. It had been my suggestion at first, but when it went up for a vote, ironically, I was the one who lobbied against it. I convinced Sarah that handsome was in the eye of the beholder, so to speak. That if you love someone, he is automatically handsome to you. Sarah argued that you needed to find someone attractive before you could fall in love with him. Not if you are of pure heart, I came back with. In the end, it was *Beauty and the Beast,* which we had both seen on Broadway, that ultimately settled things. Handsome didn't make the list, not in that form exactly.

Now Sarah nudged me and I began to read the list from the beginning.

"Number one: He must think you are the most beautiful girl in the whole wide world.

"Number two: He must say so, constantly.

"Number three: He must be smart (at least in advanced reading or higher math).

"Number four: He must . . ."

I didn't stop until I had read all that we had so far. Eleven rules for the boy we were to love, and it wasn't until I had finished all eleven that Sarah revealed her latest.

"He won't hug you; he will embrace you," Sarah said.

"What's the difference?"

Sarah sighed as if I were the most naive girl in the whole wide world. But she was my best friend, and best friends help each other out with this sort of thing.

"A hug is what your dad or mom gives you. And you give them," she tried to explain. "But an embrace . . ." Sarah suddenly stood up on her futon. She turned her back and wrapped her arms tightly around herself.

"An embrace is like all the world disappears and all there is, is you and him." She spoke into the air as if announcing a proclamation to the world. "Love will be the most wonderful thing. We will know it the minute we see him."

I jumped up beside her. "But we won't let on. . . ."

"Not right at first," Sarah added.

My face felt flushed with excitement. We stood on the futon with our arms wrapped around our shoulders, our imaginary love inhabiting our own bodies.

"No, first," I said, "we will make him . . . wait."

Sarah pretended to kiss her embracing lover, and the sight of her lips pursed into the air dropped me into a fit of giggles.

But in the end, and a mere five years later, in tenth grade, Adam matched one, maybe two, of the twenty rules Sarah and I had eventually laid out.

All that hard work. Poof. Gone in about five seconds, in about as long as it took Adam to call me "baby" for the first time, like I was something to be nurtured and taken care of. It took only for Adam to whisper that he had always thought I was beautiful and smart.

And, oh, so special.

Poof.

Because it didn't mean what I thought it would mean. None of it.

All that hard work for nothing.

* * *

Sarah doesn't know where I am. She doesn't even know about the package that came in the mail a couple of months ago.

My dad had a funny look on his face when he handed it to me. I knew even before I saw the address, the handwriting, the inside-out brown-paper-bag wrapping, the stamps, or the masking tape holding the whole thing together. I knew it was from my mother. My dad and I didn't talk about it then. Maybe we were both too much in shock, although I knew my dad had spoken with her a few times over the years. I knew my dad knew where she was, that she was OK.

But that she wasn't coming back.

At least not for the time being.

But this was the first time she was contacting me.

She had sent me a present, which I quickly stashed away in a drawer in my room. I didn't open it for a long time. It was the wrapper I was more interested in, because from it, I learned that when my mother ran away, she went to Florida.

1711 Fernando Street
St. Augustine, Florida 32084

Sarah doesn't know about any of this, but I guess it kind of fits that she doesn't. When I stopped telling Sarah *everything,* I stopped telling her anything. I didn't tell her about Adam. And then suddenly there were way too many things I hadn't told her, to tell her about the package.

Besides, sometimes I think Sarah was madder about what my mom did than I was.

So, what would Sarah think now, if she could see me sitting on this bus?

"He ain't worth it, honey."

"Huh?"

I open my eyes when I realize the lady next to me is talking to me. It was like she had been reading my mind, clicking away with her knitting needles, divining my thoughts.

"You've been crying," she says. "You're too pretty to be worried about your looks, and you're too young to be worried about money. So that leaves only one thing."

I don't say anything, but I look at her.

"Boy trouble," she says. She clicks away, metal against metal. Their sound is lost in the noise of the bus, the hum of the engine, and the thumping of the tires, and the voices of the passengers. Everyone on this bus seems to know somebody else. Or they are just more friendly than I am.

"It helps to talk about it," the lady is saying, her knitting needles clicking in a rhythmic pair.

"No, it won't," I answer, and I am looking out the window again.

"Oh, yes. It will. It always does. Sometimes, you know it's just the sound of your own voice. Just hearing it out loud. Sometimes you sound so crazy, you've just got to start laughing at yourself."

Maybe she thinks she will trick me into talking to her by doing all the talking herself.

"And sometimes, it makes you cry. But you know, I worked with this Jewish lady lawyer for a couple of years. I was a paralegal. And you know what she used to say?"

Usually my skin prickles when I hear someone talk like that: *Jewish lady*. But for some reason, this time I don't mind. It doesn't seem to mean anything. And I know she is waiting for me to ask, so I say, "What?"

"Well, she used to say, 'You laugh too hard, you cry.' It was some old Yiddish expression of her grandmother's. I think she meant that she didn't want her kids running around, getting all wild and laughing, 'cause one of them was bound to bump into something and get hurt. And start crying. You know?"

"Yeah."

"But lately I'm starting to think it means something altogether different."

"Like what?" At least she is taking my mind off of things.

"I think it means that in everything funny there's something sad and the other way around, too. Like you can't know one without knowing the other. Right?"

"I guess."

"Think about it. And talk to me when you're good and ready. We got a long trip. My backside is hurting already."

I smile. I have to.

"See, baby?" she says. "I told you."

Chapter Two

The course of true love never did run smooth.
—William Shakespeare

Adam was three years older than me. *Is* three years older, I suppose. He always will be three years older. He was in eleventh grade when I was a freshman. Now he's a senior, but he was always *different*. Before I had ever even seen Adam, I had heard this about him.

I heard that Adam Fishman is unique.

And in our high school, this is not so easy to achieve.

Redding Ridge High School prides itself on being different. Our school profile even states it. *Redding Ridge: A different kind of education*. But don't let that fool you; there really wasn't any more room to be yourself than anywhere else. In fact, being a unique individual is as much of a farce as trying to be like everyone else. Maybe more.

For some reason, a lot of famous people had moved to Redding Ridge, Connecticut, in the late eighties and early nineties. To hide, I guess. To be able to buy a pint of half-and-half in the local market without getting their picture taken. They bought big huge houses, tucked back behind big huge hills, and built big huge pools and even bigger pool houses behind those. Most of the people living in town at that time were older, retired couples who did not recognize this particular handful of famous people, not the punk-rock star with the tattoos, not the teenage movie star who had already been married twice, not the independent filmmaker who no one would have recognized anyway. Then after the famous people, the rich people started moving in.

Then *they* all started having kids. They all thought their kids were special and different.

And their kids all *felt* special and different.

Maybe they are. Everybody in my grade does something—plays an instrument, excels at some sport, sings, makes movies, writes poetry, draws, or, just as likely, all of the above. You can look any way you like, sound any way, act any way. Just so long as you don't hurt anyone, or so they say.

And still, in this eclectic mix, Adam Fishman stuck out.

And he knew it.

You got the feeling Adam was just waiting for the one person, the right girl, to match his originality, to match his spirit and honor his individuality. He certainly had a reputation for holding private auditions for the spot.

To tell the truth, until that very first time I came in contact with him, he kind of frightened me. Then that one morning, everything changed.

My dad had just dropped me off in the high-school parking lot. It was the third time I had missed my bus, and it was only my second week as a sophomore at Redding Ridge High School.

"Thanks, Dad," I said, shutting the passenger side door. I bent down and kind of waved into the window. I mouthed *sorry,* but I knew my dad never got mad at me. Never stayed mad at me.

"Don't worry. It's an adjustment," he said, and I wasn't sure if he was referring to the earlier time that the high-school bus arrived this year or our very lives.

We were the walking wounded, now four years and counting. My dad was late for work, and he drove away, leaving me in the parking lot.

Adam's car pulled up right behind me and swerved into a spot. I could hear his radio playing; his windows were all the way down. He had this weird car, an old square-style BMW that at one time might have been forest green but had faded to light pistachio, all except the right passenger door, which was a dull orange and must have once belonged to another vehicle entirely. There wasn't anything on that car that shined or reflected any light at all. And it idled loudly, like it was missing a muffler.

But it *was* unique.

"Who are you?" he said, getting out but not turning off his car engine. He said this as if he owned the school, the parking lot. Maybe the world. The radio in his car sang on. The music played into the air like a movie sound track.

He's tall, I remember thinking. Other than passing in the halls, I hadn't been this close to a senior since I got to high school. There was such a difference between the freshman and sophomore boys and the upperclassmen. Height and facial hair and voices and something else. Something about their confidence, the space they took up, the air they altered, as if they had one foot that much closer to being out the door and into the real world.

And I knew who this particular senior was. He was Adam Fishman.

"Natalie," I answered, because I figured I had to, and then added, "Gordon."

"Na-ta-lie," Adam said. He whispered it as if it were part of the song playing on his car radio. He took my hand without asking and held it high in the air. With his other hand he took the small of my back and whirled me around in time to the music. "Do you like to dance, Natalie Gordon?"

My first instinct was to pull away, to look around. To see if anyone was watching. Should I be embarrassed? Or scared? Or flattered? But there was no one around. It was late; first period must have already started. We were dancing in the parking lot, all alone. I could feel his body close to mine, so close I could smell his scent: a mixture of sweet smoke, laundry detergent, and something else, something like damp woods and cold air.

Here Adam Fishman was dancing with me and not for anyone else's benefit or joke or entertainment.

Just his.

And mine.

Her name, I find out, is Charlene. The big lady sitting next to me on the bus knitting, her name is Charlene. She's been married thirty years to the same man, a man she met at the office. She is fifty-five years old, mother of five, grandmother of eight. She's from Queens, New York, and she's on her way to visit her newest granddaughter in some town right near Newark, Delaware.

Lakeshia. That's her new granddaughter's name, not the town. Lakeshia.

With a stretch of her arm, Charlene pulls another long string from her ball of yarn. It spins a blur of purple inside her bag as it unwinds.

"So, Natalie, where did you say you were headed?"

"I didn't," I answer, but that doesn't sound nice. I have no reason to be mean. Some people just make you feel comfortable talking and listening. Charlene is one of those. I want to answer, but I don't want to tell her the truth, my story. It's too long. Too complicated. Besides, she might get worried. Call my dad or tell the driver. Or talk me out of it.

"I'm on my way to softball camp," I say. "In Florida." *Good God, where did that come from?*

"You play baseball?"

I sure as hell hope she doesn't know anything about sports.

"Softball," I correct her, if that's even possible.

"You're going by yourself?"

"Yes," I can honestly say.

Sarah wasn't hot for the whole Adam idea from the start. We were eating lunch in the cafeteria, at our favorite table, the little round one by the window. In reality we were sitting in one of the four tables relegated for underclassmen. So it was our favorite of those four, if we could get it. That day we had.

"He's a senior, Natty," she told me.

"So?" was my clever reply. "He's cool. I really like him."

"You don't even *know* him."

I knew as much as I needed to. He had chosen me.

But looking back, it is hard for me to understand what really happened. Did I like Adam, or was it simply that he liked me, which is a kind of scary thought, kind of an out-of-control idea. Because what I remember is that I suddenly felt so powerful, so *in* control, that a guy like Adam Fishman, a lacrosse-playing, hat-wearing, weird-car-driving, tall-dark-handsome (hadn't I argued against that definition once upon a time?) upperclassman, had paid attention to me, danced with me in an empty parking lot, touched my hand, the small of my back. Had looked in my eyes and called me by my name.

Na-ta-lie.

He had talked to me three times in the hall now. He even told me he had noticed me last spring at high-school orientation. He had noticed me.

That's all it took?

But yup. That's all it took.

The very last thing Sarah and I had added to our

list, before we lost interest in it and eventually lost the list somewhere between her house and mine, wasn't about boys at all. It was about girls. It was about us. And that day in the cafeteria when Sarah and I were talking, I was about to violate it, our most sacred rule of all.

Number Twenty: We will never betray each other for a boy.

"I don't know, Natty. I don't really like him," Sarah said. "He thinks he's all that."

I didn't say anything to Sarah one way or the other. I didn't agree or disagree, but in my mind, I left her. In my mind I had made a choice, right then and there. Without really realizing it, I quietly stepped over an invisible line.

I simply wouldn't tell her everything anymore.

I would no longer give my whole self up and let her in on every secret, every tiny feeling, every moment and action and observation.

We had been friends since forever, but now I was deliberately and calculatingly inching away.

And I justified the whole thing by just not paying attention, much like the cranky lunch lady who swipes somebody's lunch card without checking the name and noticing it is stolen.

From now on there would be a new place between us that only I knew about, that I controlled and from which I derived my own power, a power I was only just beginning to taste and was not willing to risk losing. I was drunk on it and I wanted to stay that way.

The first time I ever got drunk, I was with Sarah, the summer following eighth grade, right before high school, and it happened by accident. It was at Sarah's house, after one of her parents' big dinner parties. Her mother asked if Sarah and I would be willing to work, to help set up, waitress, and clean afterward.

"She'll pay us," Sarah told me. "It will be fun."

"Like playing restaurant," I added. "Remember when we used to do that?"

We were excited. Instead of being banned from the living room, dining room, and kitchen when grown-ups in their stylish clothes were around, we were invited in. We got to walk around with the guests, clear plates, fill glasses. Listen to their laughter and watch their body language, and imagine our lives as grown-ups, free and flirty, loud and liberated.

When all the guests had left, Sarah's mother let us taste the leftover champagne. Some of the people had preferred wine and left their tall, sparkling, ridiculously skinny crystal glasses full. Since Sarah and I had served and cleared, we knew exactly which ones were untouched.

We tasted quite a bit.

Being drunk is the oddest sensation. It comes on

very quickly, like a tingling warmth that starts in the center of your body and moves outward. It drifts to the mind without warning, and soon I was swimming. I was lying on the floor in Sarah's bedroom, pressed against the furry whiteness of her shaggy carpet, but I was also swimming, weightless, as if in water, moving my arms and legs around to stay afloat. There was a certain understanding that I was making a fool of myself, that my words were nonsensical and my body movements ridiculous. But there was another awareness that I was invincible, that I was powerful and special. That I was having oh, so much fun.

In those early days with Adam, that is exactly how I felt. Powerful and drunk with it. I was special. I was high.

By definition, being high means you are too far from the ground, balancing on a tightrope, hoping not to fall. Simple logic tells you no one can remain aloft forever.

High.

I became addicted to the feeling, no matter how low the crash promised to be. And the crash came pretty quickly. It came when Adam didn't return my calls quickly enough or didn't initiate a call. Or didn't phone me immediately after he left my house, left my room, left my body.

"I have such an appetite for you, Natalie," he

would whisper to me. Then in the forever moment after he was gone, I would reflect on every word he had said to me. I relived them in my imagination. I would contemplate the difference between a hunger that can be satisfied by any body and an appetite, a craving, for only one specific object. Me.

Was he thinking of me as he made his way home?

And I wanted him to acknowledge, to verbalize, that I had just shared myself with him, a very intimate part of myself.

Was he listening to the radio as he drove? A CD? Was he talking on his cell phone to a friend?

I began to wonder if I even existed for him when I wasn't directly in front of him. It was a thought that frightened me, terrified me, so that even though I knew I was making a total nag of myself, I kept calling, kept appearing before him in any way I could.

As if to say, without really saying: *Here I am.*

We were just together. As close as two people can be.

But what I would say instead, were things like: "Don't forget not to bother me when I'm watching *Grey's Anatomy* tonight." I would try to keep it light, as if I just happened to call about something else altogether, like: "Hey, did you hear what happened at the football game Saturday?"

Don't forget me. Isn't this as important to you as it is to me?

Then I would promise myself to take better care, better care of myself. Until I would see him again, and the whole cycle would repeat. I would return always to swimming drunk on champagne. And that way I didn't have to see that what I was really doing was writhing on the floor.

For a long time, I didn't have to notice that at all.

There is an old saying, a stupid, old-fashioned, ridiculous, sexist saying: You'll never sell the cow if you keep giving away the milk for free. I've heard several variations:

Why buy the cow if you can get the milk for free?

No one will pay for the milk when the cow is free.

And on and on.

Well, I wasn't trying to sell any cow. I was not, and am not, a cow, nor will I ever be one.

But for some reason that expression kept showing up in my brain like a flash card or a speed-limit sign you see as you're driving along the highway. I think there should be a better, new and improved update on that cow saying.

I'm working on it.

So while I am on a bus somewhere along Interstate 95 heading south, Sarah's family is heading north to go skiing in Vermont, and that's where my dad thinks I am. Last year, her family went to some Caribbean island for winter break, and I did get to go with them. There are actually some very good things about not having your mother around. One is that you basically get to do whatever you want.

Dads don't usually call other moms and ask them if there are enough seat belts for the drive or what the sleeping arrangements in the ski lodge are going to be. They don't even ask why I am walking out the door without a parka or some kind of huge bag to transport the skis I don't even own.

My dad gave me a hundred bucks for my week in Vermont.

"Don't spend it all in one place," he said, winking at me. He thought he was giving me a fortune, and I didn't want to burst his bubble. It's part of our walking dead routine. We never challenge each other. We never hurt each other's feelings. I tell him his cooking is great, and he tells me how special I am.

I don't think either one of us is much into telling the truth.

I tell Charlene I need to get out of my seat to get to the bathroom, but we both realize there is no way I am going to be able to squeeze by her. She's going to have to gather up all her stuff and stand up. It takes her a while to get this all organized and to get to her feet, and while she is doing this, I stand, sort of bent over, and stare at the fabric pattern of the bus seats. It is a mixture of greens and browns and aqua blue in random swirls that reminds me of vomit.

She'd better hurry.

"There you go, baby doll," Charlene says, and as I slip past, she puts her hand on the small of my back to steady me.

"I'll be right back," I say, like I should let her know this. I'm not quite sure why.

When I get inside the tiny bathroom and slide the door locked behind me, I feel a little better; the nausea passes. But now I am about to perform the same ritual I have been doing nearly every month since Adam. I take a deep breath and I pray to the God I am not sure exists and if he does I'm pretty sure he does not appreciate being used like this.

There are a million better causes in the world he is already not attending to.

But I do it anyway.

Please, I pray to God. *Let me get my period.*

Then I remember all the times before when I promised that if only I got my period, I would be more careful, next time. I would be smart. I would take more than a minor interest in my own well-being. Yet here I am again. I sit down on the toilet seat and stare into the crotch of my underpants for any sign.

We all took the same health classes, starting in middle school, didn't we? Of course, in high school they get even more interesting, more graphic, more hands-on — no pun intended. We know how to identify five different STDs, which ones are treatable and which are forever, and how to roll a condom over a rubbery penis facsimile attached to a block of wood.

Let me get my period.

After I use the toilet paper, the last part of my ritual is to inspect it for any tint, the slightest redness, the tiniest sign from God.

But there is none.

How can it be that the human brain can supposedly inhibit the growth of cancer cells or induce them? It can certainly spawn a splendid array of pimples from simple stress. Just the thought of speaking in front of a large crowd of people can send me to the bathroom with the runs.

But no matter how hard I try, I cannot will my uterus into shedding its lining.

Chapter Three

Where there is love, there is pain.
— Spanish proverb

Before I fell in love for real, I made-believe a lot.

I don't count the two boys in my kindergarten class who agreed to meet after school and fight over me, then wound up tossing a ball around the playground instead. Because my first make-believe love was Danny Bigelow, whom I kissed.

I remember Danny was pretty small, about my size, my age, eleven years old. He had sandy-colored hair to my dark brown. We were next-door neighbors, and when neither one of us had anything better to do, we hung out together. Danny and I were lying in the grass at the top of the hill by the Little League fields.

The grass was cold and a little wet. I could feel it through my sweater. My knees were bent, the sun was the most gentle blanket, and the clouds were shifting so fast against the still-bare trees that we said we could see the earth spinning.

I remember thinking, *We are either going to roll down this hill, rolling and rolling, hands tight at our sides, spinning like dizzy tops, or we are going to kiss.* There was no anticipation, no fluttering, desperate, longing feeling about it. Danny turned his head to me. Maybe he was going to challenge me to a race down the hill. Maybe he was going tell me a joke or ask me what I thought that big white cloud looked like.

So maybe it was my idea or maybe it was his. I turned my head toward Danny at the same time and our lips were a mere five inches apart. Danny leaned in the rest of the way and pressed his mouth against mine. And I pressed back. Lying on our sides, our faces touching, it was a position we held for a second or two.

His lips were soft, and his breath was sweet, like Jolly Ranchers.

After Danny and after my mother left, there was Rubin, who took me to the movies, my first real date. It was a horror movie. My dad dropped me off outside the theater. Rubin showed up a few minutes later, dropped off by his mom, who had just recently divorced Rubin's dad. I didn't realize it then, but I suppose we shared a sadness that neither one of us ever talked about.

We made out, tight-lipped, in the back row for nearly the entire duration of the film. We held hands as we left the theater, like two little kids.

Rubin moved away shortly after that, but not before we had seen two more movies and Rubin presented me with his mother's wedding ring.

I looked down at the silver circle of hearts, knowing I shouldn't accept it. I mean, he was nice and the ring was pretty; it was real. But I knew something Rubin couldn't understand. Not yet. That someday he was going to want this. Someday he was going to want to spin it around in his fingers and wonder what happened. He was going to need answers to questions he didn't yet know he was going to have, all the things that would affect his belief and trust in the world. He was going to want to read the inscription inside.

To Debbie, with all my love forever.

"No, I want you to have it," Rubin told me.

I thought I would hurt his feelings if I didn't take it. So I did.

But I certainly didn't love Rubin. And I didn't love Danny, not really. I didn't even love Taylor, who came after Rubin and before Colin. But I kissed each one of them. Rubin, I let slip his hand up my shirt, although there wasn't any part of me that understood why he would want to do that. I was determined not to laugh, although I vaguely remember hoping this wasn't what it was all about, because it tickled like crazy.

With Taylor, I learned to open my lips just slightly and let his wandering tongue invade my mouth. I learned to say hello back with mine. Colin was a freshman in high school when I was still in eighth grade. He smelled of beer, and even though I wrote his name over and over in my notebook and diary, I didn't love him either. When they were gone, they were gone. I had music to listen to, and Sarah to talk to. I had books to read and magazine pictures to look at. I had homework and tests and essays to write, posters to draw, and movies to watch. I wrote poetry and short stories that nobody read but me, and that was enough. I swam and ran and danced when no one was looking because I wanted to.

And that had once been enough.

In Spanish you can say, *Te amo,* which means "I love you."

But you can also say *Te quiero*.

Amo comes from the verb "to love," *amar,* whereas *quiero* comes from the verb *querer,* meaning "to want."

Te quiero. "I want you."

I want you. I love you. I need you to want me.

I know there is a significant difference here; I am just not sure what it is.

So along with that arguably unflattering expression about cows and milk, I am subsequently working on this.

We've been rolling along about two hours since we left New York City, and I think we're still in New Jersey. The bus is filling with the odors of food. It seems everyone has brought something in Tupperware or tinfoil. First it's the noise: the crinkling of metallic paper and unsnapping of hard plastic tops. And then the smells: potato chips, barbecue sauce, fried chicken, cheese puffs, pickles. I swear I smell the cheese puffs.

Charlene is unwrapping what looks like a bologna sandwich spread with mayonnaise, which seems to me a culinary violation, at least in my Jewish family.

"Please take half," she says.

"Oh, no, thanks." I wave her away, but this doesn't even slow her down.

"I won't eat unless you eat with me."

She seems to have a great deal of food with her in her tapestry bag on the floor between her feet. She hands me the half sandwich, still in its wrapper.

"OK, thanks." I smile and I chew slowly. Actually the food helps my stomach a bit.

"So what position do you play?" Charlene asks me.

"Play?"

"Softball. What position do you play?"

"Um. I play first base," I say, and then, because a good lie requires just enough detail, I add, "And I pitched a little until I hurt my shoulder."

Charlene is opening a plastic container of celery and carrot sticks. She holds the container right over my lap so I have no choice. "I always have extra of these with me. I'm on a diet," she tells me.

"That's good," I say. I take a carrot, but then I wonder if that didn't sound right.

Charlene doesn't seem to mind. She says, "I played softball in college."

"Really?" I turn away and look out the window. *Oh, shit.*

The bus has slowed slightly with the traffic. It is very flat here, and for the most part, the highway is segregated by a tall privacy wall, made of what looks like giant Lincoln Logs. But every so often there is a break, and I can see a house or two, set as if they are peeking through, watching, not wanting to miss anyone driving by. One is still sadly dressed in bleached-out Christmas decorations. A soot-covered reindeer and Santa sit on top of its roof.

"Do you know where we are?" I ask Charlene. All I can do is try and change the subject. I've already used up everything I know about sports.

Charlene leans forward a bit and looks past me through the window as if she is assessing the geography. "We are right about here," she says with a laugh. "Yup. We are right here."

The sun is at high noon, filtered through the dirty window glass and spreading across my lap and face. I don't see any people out the window, just little glimpses through the empty spaces: a rusty swing set, a bicycle frame beside a tree, trash cans, a driveway with an orphaned snowplow sitting on its side. All the manifestations of the human beings I imagine live around here.

"No, seriously, I don't know, sweetheart," Charlene goes on. "I've moved around a lot. I have since I was about your age."

It's really hard for me to imagine that this tremendous woman was once my age, but I have to assume she was.

"I've learned to enjoy the trip," she says. "You know what I mean?"

Something about what Charlene says makes me look down at my cell phone again. There is no message icon blinking. I flip it open and check missed calls, just to make sure. I check my reception bars and then my missed calls again. I think about calling for my messages to make double sure, but Charlene is watching me. I feel her thoughts, as if they are pressed upon my body.

He was dark. Darker than she was. So dark she could see the shot of red in the white of his eyes. The color of his eyes, so dark she couldn't see their centers. The palms of his hands seemed to glow in the night, moving across her body. His lips were like warmth itself. Charlene had never felt so beautiful. She had, in fact, never felt beautiful before.

"We barely know each other," she whispered. Her parents were sleeping. They were sleeping in the upstairs bedroom. This house was incredible, so open. The warm air, the constant breezes, the smell of flowers and rain drifting in through the wide-open shades, the lifted screens. There were porches off every door, where the ocean rose and fell, calling out, even when it couldn't be directly seen.

The sand was pure white. The sky was a new color entirely, cobalt blue. The house was peach with turquoise storm shutters. Jamaica was like a storybook. It was as if you took the East Bronx, put it in a dictionary, and tried to find its exact opposite, its polar self. The farthest place from everything Charlene had ever known or seen, or smelled or tasted or heard.

"I know *you,*" he whispered back. "I've been watching you for days. I have such an appetite for you, Charlie."

Even though those words rang in her mind like lyrics to a song that someone else wrote, she let them be sung to her. His accent like music, his name was Eldon.

There must be a reason, Charlene thought, that her dad won this trip. His promotion at work, a week in Jamaica, a private house on the beach. A cook. And Eldon, who had been introduced to them by the real estate lady, as the "house boy" as he carried their luggage into the house.

Nothing like this happens by accident. Some people were meant to find each other, even across an ocean.

And to think, at first she hadn't wanted to go.

I don't care if Daddy won some stupid vacation at his boss's house. I won't know anybody. I can stay home alone. You and Daddy and Trevor can go. I don't want to go. There won't be anyone my age. You can't make me go.

Charlene had tested into the Bronx High School of Science, and her parents made her attend. Every day she was surrounded by bone-china–skinned Asian kids and super-smart white kids from Manhattan, who came in throngs off the subway each morning, and only three kids from her own neighborhood, all boys. And not only that but she had also moved up a grade years ago, making her only fifteen years old and a senior in high school. She was too smart, too young, and too dark, and none of those things equaled beauty.

Until now. Until Eldon.

"I love you," he told her. He slipped his hand under her shirt, and the remarkable feel of his skin on her skin — on her back, on her belly, on her ribs — took her breath away.

"You are so beautiful" over and over with his singsongy accent.

He also told her he had never seen a black family staying in this house where he worked. Families came and went, some tipped more than others, but the one constant was that they were all white as ghosts. Until Charlene.

Until you.

Her blackness was beauty here. It seemed destined to stand out against the turquoise sky and the white, white sand. In Jamaica, where everyone was dark, darker and even darker than that, she was a vision. Her hair was beauty here. Her lips, her nose. She didn't have to stare in the mirror as she did back home, searching to match the words she would say to the face she saw. *Black is beautiful. Black is beautiful.*

Here, it was unspoken. Here it simply was, and always had been.

Here was Eldon, and she melted into the beauty that was power. Into the power that was belief. Into the belief that this was love.

When Charlene tells me she's getting off here, just before we cross over the bridge, my stomach twists into a familiar, unpleasant sort of discomfort.

"I thought you were going to Delaware," I say for some reason. "This is still New Jersey."

Mount Laurel, the driver just announced.

"I know, baby, but it's closest. My nephew Ralphie is picking me up here."

She is already gathering her belongings, her knitting, her paperback book, her packages of food.

I have never been good at saying good-bye. Never. But it strikes me as odd that I feel this way about a woman I met three hours ago. A woman I will never see again. I mean, I guess there's a chance, but the odds are millions, billions to one that our lives will cross again. So why?

Why do I feel anxious that she is leaving?

And sad.

"Look, little lady," she is saying to me. She is standing in the aisle. No one else, it seems, is getting off here. The whole bus is waiting, but Charlene doesn't seem to care. She talks as slowly and for as long as she wants. I like that about her. You've got to admire that.

"You take care of that shoulder now," she says.

"What?"

"Your pitching arm." She smiles at me. "And the whole rest of yourself, when you figure that out."

"Right," I say.

"You know what I'm talking about." But she doesn't move away. "Stand up now," Charlene orders me.

I do, and she puts her arms around me. She smells like floral perfume, and when I look at her face, really look at her, I see she is beautiful. Sometimes I am uneasy hugging people, grown-ups especially, but Charlene doesn't have any room for that. She does all the hugging, and she does the letting go when she's good and ready.

"I'll take care of myself. I will, Charlene," I tell her. "I promise you."

The driver had gotten off the bus to get her suitcase out. Now he's waiting by the door, waiting to get going again, like everyone else on the bus.

"Don't promise *me,* girl," Charlene says.

And she is gone.

Along with the hum of the bus engine, the smells of food, and human bodies too long without fresh air, I am alone again, and I allow myself to drift into a daydream world of partial memories and partial fantasy, all involving Adam, until the bus begins to lurch in a series of staccato spasms.

I wonder if there is something wrong with the bus.

I try to ignore this and linger in the feeling of Adam touching me while it is still alive in my mind. My skin tightens and trembles as if it is real, even as my brain and my heart know it is not.

This bus is really making odd noises.

I open my eyes and look out the window as the driver pulls off the highway at the first exit. The bus slows to a stop along a busy stretch of the service road. I see a bunch of gas stations and two fast-food restaurants, a video store, a Kmart, and across the street is a diner that sits slightly apart. OUR DOG HOUSE, the sign on the roof reads.

It looks like a house really, a house with a trailer attached and a sign on its roof in the shape of a giant hot dog.

Chapter Four

Love is like butter; it's good with bread.

—Yiddish proverb

The driver tells us he needs to stop the bus. He tells us not to get off, he'll only be a minute, and if something is wrong he'll radio for another bus. But after about ten minutes with the sun beating through the windows, a bunch of people get up anyway and are standing around the side of the road.

I am one.

I should probably call my dad, but I don't have a good enough signal. As I walk toward the end of the bus and then a little more toward the street, I get another bar on my cell phone.

It turns out I get the best reception right inside Our Dog House, which it turns out *is* somebody's house with a trailer attached. The trailer part is the diner. There is a long counter with stools and some booths against the far wall. There is one person working: a young girl behind the counter.

Now I can call my dad and pretend I am on my way to Vermont. I know parents like to think that cell phones have allowed them to keep better track of their teenagers, but they are always a few steps behind.

My dad doesn't answer, so better still, I leave a message and then shut my phone off to save power.

"You gonna order something?" The girl behind the counter talks to me.

And suddenly I realize I am nauseous, or hungry again. All I've had is half a bologna sandwich and a carrot stick since six thirty this morning.

"Yeah," I answer, taking a seat on one of the round red stools.

The waitress hands me a menu, but I already know what I want, and I order it. It is what I always order in a place like this: grilled cheese on white and a chocolate milk shake. My mom and I used to get the exact same thing every time we went to the diner on the post road in Westport on my way to Hebrew school. Every Wednesday for two years, grilled cheese and a chocolate milk shake. She got the same thing, except she had tomato on her grilled cheese, and instead of a milk shake she got a chocolate egg cream, which has neither eggs nor cream.

"You know what?" I say suddenly. "Can I change that? Can I have an egg cream instead? Chocolate?"

"A what?"

I forgot. You don't have to go too far out of the tristate area before no one has ever heard of an egg cream. I read the signs as we crossed the state lines. Delaware for a split second and now we are in Maryland. No egg creams.

"Nah, forget it. I'll just have water."

As the waitress is talking to me, I realize she probably isn't much older than I am. I'm almost sixteen. Maybe she's seventeen. Maybe. She seems kind of unhappy to be where she is, which is OK because I am feeling pretty much the same.

"Grilled cheese and a water . . ." She hurries off to take someone else's order.

I am just sitting, letting my knees knock against the back of the counter, letting the stool rock one way and then the other, waiting for my sandwich. The stool makes a funny squeaking sound when it spins left and a thunking noise when it stops forward again. I'd liked going to Hebrew school, which is pretty weird in itself. Maybe I just liked the special time with my mom. I had her all to myself. There were no phones to answer. She couldn't go lie down in her room with the door shut. She couldn't fight with my dad or stare at the TV. She'd ask me about school, about my homework, my friends.

I remember I thought she was the most beautiful woman in the world. I wanted to be just like her. She had long hair—blond, kind of thin and wispy. Pieces of it would be lifted upward at the slightest wind. When the afternoon light came right in through the large windows by our booth, her hair would look like a halo. She was tiny, my mom. Thin, small-boned. Tiny, like you wanted to pick her up and carry her away. Frail, like she *wanted* to be picked up and carried away.

Not like me at all.

I was never tiny. I am tall, but not because I have long, modelly legs. I am just tall. I wore a size eight-and-a-half shoe by the time I was in eighth grade. I was born with a thick head of dark brown hair that just got thicker and curlier every year.

I'm pretty sure I was born big.

One thing I do know for certain: I was born by mistake.

If it hadn't been so hard to find, I might have thought that my mother left this one thing behind on purpose. I might have thought I was meant to find it. It was just a month or so after she left.

At first glance it was just a shoe box; size five shoe,

my mother's tiny feet. Dented cardboard. Color: rich brown.

Sarah and I had to make a diorama for sixth-grade American History. We hadn't gotten to choose our subject. We had to make a visual representation of the *Bon Homme Richard,* which is a boat or a battle or a revolutionary war hero, and that's about all we knew. We had some old Playmobil army figures, miniature British and American flags, and a crude silhouette of an eighteenth-century battleship made of paper, and now we needed a box to house our miniature project.

"Here," I said.

"Where?"

"There." I was pointing far into the recesses of my dad's closet. Way in the back, in the places you never look unless you had waited the entire three weeks to begin a project that was now due tomorrow and you were desperate.

Sarah was on the floor, poking around, and I was on a chair, looking on the top shelf of the closet. I could see, behind all the old suits, a stack of boxes hidden by a pile of old sweaters.

"Where?" she asked again, looking up.

"Wait, I see it. I'll get it." I stretched onto my tippy-toes. I closed my eyes and turned my head so I could get my arm in as far as it would go and pulled out a cardboard box. Our project was only another half an hour or so to completion. Sarah smiled and took the box from my hands.

"But it's got stuff in it," she said. She had lifted the lid.

"So what?" I said. "We'll throw it out, or we can stuff it back in the closet again. Nobody's looked back there in about a hundred years." I figured it was an old pair of shoes or a nasty holey sweater, old ties. Something like that.

"Yeah, funny, a hundred years, like since John Paul Jones." Sarah laughed.

"Who?"

She shot me a look that said she had done *her Bon Homme Richard* research and I had not. But I owned the old Playmobil toys and I had drawn the paper boat, so fair's fair.

It seemed like the contents were just old envelopes and yellowing papers, but when I looked closer, I saw official-looking documents. The one on the very top as I lifted it all was folded into thirds, facing out. *Department of Health Services,* it read. *License and Certificate of Marriage*.

Sarah looked from the paper to my face and back again. She was one of the only people who knew about my mother. Sarah and, of course, my grandmother, and my father's best friend, Joel, Uncle Joel. But surprisingly it never came up. The school didn't really know. Teachers didn't know.

A Gordon family don't-ask-don't-tell policy. And they never really asked.

It makes it easy. People don't ask about what they don't really want to know. People don't really want to know what doesn't involve or matter to them. My dad came in for all the conferences, the plays. He signed all my permission slips and report cards.

We just became a family of two, instead of three.

No biggie.

I unfolded the paper while Sarah read over my shoulder.

Legal fee: $3.00—Certified Copy was stamped across the whole thing. I let my eyes wander over the words, the dates, the ages. Maiden name. County of. City of. Education. My mother was twenty-three years old. My dad was thirty-four. They were married May 19th. I guess I knew that. I remembered the anniversary gifts. Flowers. Babysitters. Dinner out. Dinner in.

It was Sarah who brought it up.

"Hey, isn't your birthday in November?" she said.

"Yeah."

"So look, your parents were married only six months before you were born." And then she stopped, like she had said something wrong. But I still didn't get it.

"So?"

"Nothing."

I folded the paper back up and took the whole handful, and I was about to shove it back into the closet. I wanted to get back to the American Revolution and John Paul Jones, who said, "Give me liberty or give me death." Or maybe he said, "I regret I have but one life to live for my country." Or maybe he didn't say anything. Maybe he just dropped dead.

Oh.

I got it.

My mother was three months pregnant when she got married. She had never wanted to get married in the first place. She had to. So much for love. My mother had never wanted me. Maybe that's what she was trying to tell me that day.

I was a mistake, one mistake that led to another.

No wonder she left.

I finally got it.

When my grilled cheese comes, there are three crinkle-cut pickle slices on the plate beside it. And the sandwich itself looks a little flatter, a lot greasier than I think I can handle right now. More like a slice of pizza than a sandwich, and I don't feel the least bit hungry anymore.

"You don't like it?" the waitress asks, the way a mother would, which strikes me as sort of funny but nice; she's just a kid like me. I guess being a waitress is like being a mother, sort of. With tips.

"Oh, no. I'm just not as hungry as I thought."

Then as if my answer were an invitation, the waitress leans back against the sliding-glass doors of the dessert display right behind her. She lets out a long sigh, almost a parody of exhaustion.

If this girl had a cigarette, I imagine she'd be smoking. She kind of looks like the type of girl who smokes.

"So," she says to me. "Where are you going?"

"Going?" I ask. I turn around to look out the window. I can see the bus and even more passengers lined up along the street. *Maybe nowhere,* I think.

"Yeah, well, everybody who comes in here is going somewhere. If you lived around here, you'd know better. Plus, I know pretty much everybody from here."

"Florida," I say. "To see my mother."

Back at school, there were always those girls who started smoking early, the skinny ones with black eyeliner and belly rings who gathered in the parking lot before first period. The black nail polish type. Although they'd surprise you. Sometimes you'd see a cheerleader out there, or an honor student blackening her lungs with seductive tendrils of smoke. It keeps you skinny, they tell me.

The waitress smiles. "I wish I could go to Florida."

"Yeah?"

"I'd go anywhere," she says. "But I can't."

That's when I notice the ring on her finger, on her third finger, left hand. A wedding band. She walks away to give someone their check, and when she comes back, she returns to the same spot and exact stance, as if she stands there a hundred times a day. Arms folded, ankles crossed, leaning directly in front of the slices of pie, bowls of rice pudding, and half globes of cantaloupe covered in cellophane.

I still haven't touched my sandwich, and I don't want her to ask me about it again. So I say, "Are you married?"

She looks down at her hand. She spreads her fingers and sort of wiggles them around.

"Yup."

"That's nice." *How lame can I be?*

"You don't mean that," she says, but she isn't angry. She steps toward the counter and leans on her elbows. She looks tired.

"No, I do. I mean . . ." I go on. "I think if you really love someone, you can meet them now just as easily as later, right? I mean, how do you know?"

"You don't," she says.

I started feeling that this girl could have just been one of my friends, even with all that blue eye shadow, even with that wedding ring. Maybe we rode the school bus together for years. We were never in any of the same classes and didn't see each other outside of school, but we are really close friends. Summer friends. And neighborhood friends. Or just bus friends.

Oh, right, my bus is outside.

I wonder if it's fixed yet, or what?

"Hey, can I just take this with me?" I say suddenly.

"Sure, I'll wrap it up," she says, sliding the plate back toward her. "By the way, I'm Lorraine."

"I'm Natalie," I say, turning my head to look again out the window, the window that looks out across the highway, to the gas stations and the video store, the doughnut chain and the pancake house, and I watch as a long silver bus, the one with the picture of the running dog on the side, the one on its way from Connecticut to Florida, gathers speed and moves off with the flow of traffic.

Lorraine sat and watched the PBS special flicker on the screen in the darkened classroom. "There are fifteen different words for snow in the Eskimo language," the narrator began. "Snowflake, frost, fine snow, drifting particles, clinging particles, fallen snow on ground . . ."

And so on.

Lorraine let herself fall into the movie as the camera passed over the frozen, nearly bluish glaciers, dipping and rising along the rounded formations. She was tired in a way she had never been before. After weeks of running to the bathroom between every class, even getting up in the middle of the night to check for her period, for drops of red, Lorraine finally bought a test kit—the most expensive, most accurate one. She had driven two towns over to find a pharmacy where no one would know her.

The results had been pink—positive.

Lorraine knew now (no matter what she decided to do about this) that she was forever separate from her classmates, though she could hear them talking behind her. When they realized their teacher was absent, most of the kids had cut out completely. The rest were fooling around in the back of the room. One kid even lit up a cigarette. The substitute teacher that day was too afraid to say anything. She just sat there pretending to be really interested in the documentary.

And so on.

Crust on fallen snow. Fresh fallen snow on the ground. Fallen snow floating on water. There was whiteness everywhere, falling from the sky, suspended in the wind. "There could be no one single word for something as important as snow," the narrator went on. "It would be like a human infant being referred to just as 'baby' for his or her entire life. Language defines culture."

Lorraine instinctively reached down and rubbed her belly. It was flat. Flat as it ever had been. It seemed nearly impossible, and yet, of course, it was entirely possible.

Three more kids left the room. Lorraine turned around and watched them go. The room brightened when they slipped out, then returned to darkness with the click of the shutting door. Dust hung suspended in the long beam of light that stretched from the projector to the screen. Lorraine let her eyes settle into a blur, staring at the movie.

"For example," the voice intoned, "do we call a buttercup a weed or a flower?"

A weed or a flower?

"Is it defined by its beauty or its wildness?"

What words would define me now? Lorraine thought. Carson had used the word *love*. He had told her he loved her many times. There should really be at least a few more words for love in the English language. Maybe it would help clear things up a little. Prevent these kinds of things from happening.

Certainly the love she felt for her parents was a different love altogether from the love she felt for Carson. And the love she had for reading and dreaming of all the places she would travel. Perhaps the love Carson felt for her was just slightly different from the love she felt for him. If there had been another word, a more perfect word, maybe things would be better understood. Suddenly, Lorraine felt unbelievably hungry, almost a burning, though she knew no food would be satisfying.

The movie ended.

"Will somebody get the lights?" the sub called out, and when the room lit up again, she acted surprised that there were only five kids left in the room. She kept shaking her head as she handed out the worksheet questions.

"To be completed in class today."

Lorraine looked down at the paper on her desk. What would happen to her next? Even if she skipped ahead, past telling her parents and grandparents, and friends, what would happen? She clicked the lead down into her mechanical pencil but didn't write anything.

The bell rang.

"Everyone turn in your work sheets," the sub called out loudly, as if she were still talking to an entire class. Lorraine wrote her name at the top of the paper and turned it in, completely blank.

Chapter Five

In love there
are two things:
bodies and words.
—Joyce Carol Oates

Your *what* is leaving? Your bus?" Lorraine is talking to me, but I can barely hear her.

My head is starting to hurt, as if I've had this horrible headache and I am only now just realizing it. I feel my heart start to tighten with fear, the little-kid kind of fear, where everything looms large.

I am stuck here in . . . where am I?

Lorraine tells me I am in Craigstown, Maryland. *Where?* Dear God. Now surely I am going to cry. Or throw up. I feel suddenly nauseous again, only more so.

"What am I going to do?" I am asking no one in particular. I think I am shouting.

"That was your bus?" Lorraine asks.

"That was my bus."

"To Florida?" Now she is shouting as well.

I nod.

"Oh, shit."

Now we are both quiet. There are only a few other people in the diner. There is a man five stools down from me, and an older couple, a man and woman in a booth by the window, and they all seem interested in my dilemma, like they've got nothing better to do.

They probably don't.

My mouth is opening and closing like a fish. My mind is clicking into place, sorting through my limited options.

Giving up, calling my dad.

Getting to the nearest bus station and buying another ticket.

Money. I wouldn't have enough to get home.

Calling Adam?

Ha. Good one.

Giving up and calling my dad.

Fainting.

Fainting may turn out to be my best alternative after all. I can feel the blood rushing to my head, or away from it. My fingers are starting to tingle.

"Maybe you can catch up to them," Lorraine says, and we both look out the window at the traffic. The bus is stopped at an intersection about an eighth of a mile ahead. Red taillights blink on and off. I can see the entrance signs to Interstate 95 and for a long second I have an image of myself as one of those superheroes in cartoons who run really fast, a blur of color streaking behind.

I look back at Lorraine.

"I mean, get a ride or something," she says. "Does the bus stop again?"

The schedule.

Yes, I think. The bus does stop. I remember. In New York City, New York. In Baltimore, Maryland. In Richmond—

"Yes, in Baltimore," I say quickly. "Is that near here?"

Lorraine nods. "Sort of."

"Hey, Del. Ain't you going to Baltimore?" the man beside me at the counter says out loud. He looks like something out of one of those save-the-farm movies. He is white, with a wrinkled face, dirty overalls, and a John Deere cap on his head. He is talking to the couple in the booth. He pronounces *Baltimore* as though it were only two syllables and with no *T*: *Bal'more.*

The man in the booth doesn't say anything but nods his head up and down, for an extended amount of time. I guess he is going to Baltimore.

"That's a bad neighborhood over there by the bus

station," the female half of the booth couple says. I am not sure who she is talking to, but my bus must surely be driving farther and farther away every second.

"All the more reason for you and Del to drive the girl there," Mr. John Deere says.

"Suppose we could do that," the woman agrees. "We have to go there anyway."

I look to Lorraine, since I've run out of people in the room who I can understand.

"That's very nice of you, Mrs. Johnson," Lorraine says slowly.

Everything is looming large.

Much too large. You feel all alone, like a little kid, only your mom is not coming to pick you up.

My mother left a lot of times before she left for real. All those other times, I never realized what she was doing.

But she was practicing.

For a while, I thought there was something I could do to stop her; that it was my choice, my fault. The first time it happened we were in a big store. In my memory, I am in the child seat of a metal shopping cart. There are tall shelves and aisles like highways, one of those massive warehouse stores you have to be a member of to shop in.

But that could be just a memory. I was not quite four years old.

I wanted to get out of that cart in a bad way, kicking my legs, letting my feet fly up into my mother's chest and stomach. Gripping the bar tightly until the top of my hands were red, then white. Screaming, probably saying something to the effect of *Let me out.*

I want to get down.

Down.

I wanted to see something, something this moving shopping cart had passed by and hadn't allowed me a good look at: a cartoon character on a cereal box, a colorful package of candy. I don't remember anymore. What I do remember is the feeling of being wheeled away against my will, trapped and stuck. I started to lift my knees out of the cart anyway, with no sense of gravity or concept of height. I had no sense that I could get hurt.

Because you can't get hurt when you are with your mother.

Stop, Natty.

Sit still, please.

Be good, my mother would have said quietly. She never yelled.

I clearly remember the cold metal and the sense of frustration when I couldn't get my legs out by myself.

I needed to jiggle myself free, or make enough of a stink to be lifted out.

Finally my mother let me down, and as soon as she did, I darted off down the aisle back toward the object of my desire, the cereal box or the candy. I looked back once, to see if she was right behind me. I froze at the sight of my mother turning the corner and heading away from me.

And in an instant she was gone.

I was old enough to realize that it was more logical for me to continue forward and speed around the top of the next aisle to see her again. This I did, the black-and-white tiles under my feet like a monstrous checkerboard. I quickly turned the corner, around the cookie display, but she wasn't there.

She wasn't in this aisle. Or this one.

Not this one. Not this one. Not this one.

I was running as fast as I could. Fast. Running. The towers of boxes and colors blurring beside me. The checkout lines were miles long, crowded with strange faces and cart after cart after cart, all looking like ours.

I was crying by that time. Hysterical. So much snot was running down my face, I could taste it, mixed salty with my crying. I didn't care. I was blinded with pooling, seeping, drowning tears and the fear, the enormous out-of-control realization that I was truly lost.

A woman who smelled like maple syrup picked me up, and the rest is a confusion of sights, people, an office, discussions, a loudspeaker. Someone gave me a drink of water. And then my mother was there.

Here you go, little girl. See, I told you there was nothing to worry about. Here's your mommy.

My mother looked happy to see me but certainly calm.

I remember thinking, *She isn't crying*.

The inside of the Johnsons' truck smells like gasoline and wood. Beside me, in the back, an old gray army blanket is draped across the seat. It itches me when I lean on it. The dashboard is covered with what looks like invoices and receipts, and several old coffee-stained Styrofoam cups. I like it. I look out the window. I am riding in a car with total strangers. I have been warned about this all my life.

Only Mrs. Johnson seems to know how to speak.

She is telling me about the time she went to New York City. The Big Apple, she calls it.

She came up to see the lights at Rockefeller Center and the Christmas Spectacular at Radio City Music Hall.

Had I seen it? How lucky. Did I do all my Christmas shopping on Fifth Avenue?

I think better than to tell her nobody shops on Fifth Avenue except for tourists, or that I'm Jewish and don't have Christmas.

What am I doing in this truck?

I check my cell phone for calls. Voice message? Text? Nothing.

What am I doing?

Lorraine had assured me it was perfectly safe. She's known the Johnsons all her life. She went to school with their kids and their cousins' kids. Her husband works for a construction company and they just put a roof up for the Johnsons, just this last summer. But it was all pretty strange, since I didn't know Lorraine either.

We hugged good-bye, as if we were old friends.

"You said the bus has an hour layover in Baltimore," she told me. "Don't worry. You have plenty of time."

"Thanks for helping me," I told her.

"I didn't do anything. I mean, I wish I could. I'd drive you myself, but my car is in the shop, as usual."

I looked around and noticed that another waitress had come in at some point and was wiping the counter where I had been sitting.

"That's OK. That would be crazy. I think it's pretty far . . . like half an hour, right?"

Lorraine nodded. "Yeah, but it would be an

adventure, right? I hardly leave here. I hardly never go anywhere."

"I suppose," I said, smiling, and I got in with the Johnsons, who had pulled up outside Our Dog House.

I didn't realize I had forgotten my grilled cheese until I looked back and saw Lorraine waving with one hand, holding a paper bag in the other, but it was too late.

"Put your seat belt on."

Mr. Johnson's voice startles me. We've been driving for about ten minutes already, in total silence, but it is as if her husband's voice awakens her, and Mrs. Johnson starts telling me about her aunt Judy, who tried out for the Rockettes herself.

"What?" I say.

"The Rockettes," Mrs. Johnson says to me. "At Radio City."

"No, I mean . . . oh, sorry. My seat belt."

Mr. Johnson watches me in his rearview mirror as I reach around and pull up the floppy cloth seat belt. It takes me another minute to adjust it and snap it into place.

Mr. Johnson doesn't say another thing the rest of the ride, but his wife tells me about her younger brother, Troy, who married a girl from Troy, New York.

Can you believe that one? They have three kids of their own and seven grandchildren.

And now they all live in Buffalo.

Have I ever been to Buffalo?

How about Arizona? The Johnsons went to Arizona once to see the Grand Canyon.

Adam never wore a seat belt.

Never.

And before Adam, I had never gotten into a car and *not* automatically fastened my seat belt. It was like second nature, just something I did. So at first, I didn't even notice that Adam wasn't wearing his. He let his wrist rest limply on the top of his steering wheel. His other arm, he draped on my shoulder. I felt like a princess. He leaned back, not like my father, who drove sitting straight up, eyes ahead. My dad kept two hands on the wheel most all the time, and if he only used one, at least it was with a firm grip.

When Adam turned the car, he did it with only the palm of his hand, as if gripping the wheel was a sign of weakness, too much bother, or both.

I melted.

And the next time I got into the car with him, I reached for my seat belt and then stopped. I let it drop instead. Adam didn't say anything. The car moved forward, and I tried to ignore the odd sensation of being unbelted, unencumbered. It felt uncomfortable, unsafe, wrong. But I persevered.

And soon I liked it.

I was free.

Sometimes, Adam would lean over and kiss me while he was driving. His tongue probing my mouth.

I hesitated.

"You're driving. Don't." I giggled.

I'd never giggled before, had I? But I didn't pull away. I didn't get out of the car. I didn't even reach over and snap my seat belt into place; this was dangerous. Instead, I leaned toward him as closely as I could, hoping this would enable him to still see the road. But all and all, I gave *him* the choice, the control. I turned over my free will to Adam Fishman, and it made me feel like a precious, fragile china doll.

The problem was he didn't quite see it the same, did he?

I can still hear his male voice, urging, demanding. *Give me your tongue. Let me feel your tongue,* he'd whisper into my mouth. His torso stretched across the seat, his hand pressing against the back of my head, telling me what to do.

And I would do it.

Mr. Johnson spoke only one more time, as I was getting out of the backseat of their truck. He had pulled right in front of the bus station, nearly up on the curb so I would have only a few steps, walking directly through the glass doors and safely inside. Although, to tell the truth, the inside of the bus station didn't look all that much better than the outside.

"Stay out of trouble," Mr. Johnson said. It was the same tone he used to tell me to put my seat belt on.

It was a fatherly thing to say. I don't think he meant anything in particular by it, but it suddenly struck me as funny. Stay out of trouble. Aren't I in trouble already?

Isn't that what it used to be called, when a guy got a girl pregnant?

He got her in trouble.

As if she had very little to do with it, a passive bystander. Now *she* was in trouble, but he was not. He had only gotten her there; the rest was her problem.

"I will," I told him. "Thank you both so much for the ride."

Then just before I step inside, I look up at the sky. It is threateningly dark. I wonder if it snows down here, but it doesn't feel cold enough. It is damp and chilly, and I begin to feel a low dull cramp, a pleasant heaviness that makes my heart quicken.

Chapter Six

You, yourself, as much as anybody in the entire universe, deserve your love and affection.

—Buddha

The bathroom of the Baltimore bus station is disgusting. Beyond disgusting. Not only do I have three layers of toilet paper folded over the seat, but I am squatting with all my leg strength, while holding the stall door closed with one hand, since it seems to be missing a lock. Where the lock may have once been is a perfect circle, like the porthole of a ship, except that the only thing I can see out this window is a row of dirty sinks strewn with wet paper towels. I am holding on and trying to release at the same time.

This takes so much effort that I almost don't see it.

Red.

Like the swirl of color inside a marble.

Blood.

A swell of relief surges through my body as I stand up.

I rub my belly, my womb, as if to thank her for forgiving my stupidity yet another month. Does this really make the fourth month in a row that I made unkept promises to myself? My immense gratitude and another set of renewed vows to take better care of myself last only long enough for me to realize that I suddenly have a great urge to call Adam.

I want to call Adam.

Just to let him know, I think.

There is some logic in this, I rationalize instantaneously. The way you might scratch an itch that hasn't yet registered in your mind as irritating.

I need to hear his voice. And now I have something good to tell him. I'll sound cheerful and upbeat. I'll have good news. Good news for him.

I got "it," I can hear myself saying already. I rehearse my words in my mind, and I feel excited just thinking about it. I walk out into the lobby of the station, and I don't even wait to find a more private spot to make my call.

I check my cell phone for reception bars as I force out any thoughts that this is a bad idea, that if it doesn't go well, I will feel worse than before I called. He could be busy, or uninterested. Or worse. Much worse.

But of course, there is always a chance he'll be wonderful and loving, and kind and concerned. And I will feel so much better.

In this ridiculous debate, the desire to feel better wins out.

I call.

I can feel the excitement just pressing the buttons of his cell phone number.

"Hello?" Adam answers on the first ring. I pretend he has been waiting for my call.

"Hello," I say back.

"Natty?" As his voice moves through me, an image is formed. My brain races to put the scene together based on the background sounds, the tone, the exact words.

Where is he? Is he alone?

He is smiling. I can hear it in his voice — a warm summer rain that has just ended, revealing a wet and glistening world, and I know he would like the analogy.

"Natalie." He says it again, more softly. And I know he is alone. He wouldn't talk like that in front of his friends.

"Hi," I say, lowering my voice. Trying to sound as intimate, as if I am not surrounded by transient, rushing, waiting, loud-talking, bus-traveling strangers. I walk around searching for a more private area, but still concentrating all of my attention on this conversation, hoping to steer it in the right direction.

Then, suddenly, Adam isn't saying anything.

Are you there? I want to ask in a panic, but I know him. He is pausing, forcing my hand, forcing me to talk, to fill in the silence and betray myself as needy. It is like two people holding on to opposite ends of a rope.

I hear nothing in the phone.

In order to keep the line taut, one person has to keep pulling. Or the rope will fall. Why is it always me?

But it is.

"So where are you?" I ask, breaking into the anxious quiet, and giving myself away.

"Home." And he pauses again. I can feel the pull drawing me in, like air into a bell jar.

"So what are you up to?" he asks.

I realize Adam doesn't even know I've left. He doesn't know that I'm not in town, not in my home, not at Sarah's, not with my dad. I am on the road, hours and hours away. He doesn't know that I crossed the Mason-Dixon line over ninety minutes ago.

And Adam hasn't been waiting around for my "good" news, has he?

I got it.

He has not been waiting month after month, day after day. In fact, my menstrual cycle is probably not foremost in his thoughts. He has been with his friends having a beer, or watching TV, at practice, or eating breakfast, lunch, dinner with his parents and brothers.

No, if I tell him, he won't even know what I'm talking about.

"So are you busy? Where *are* you?" he asks again. I know he wants to see me. Now. I have to change the subject. Distract him, letting him think that the possibility of seeing me is still real, even though it is not.

It is surprisingly easy not to answer Adam if I don't want to. All I have to do is ask him something about himself. He falls for it every time.

"Are you in your room?" I ask.

"I am," he says slowly. "I wish you were with me."

I feel my heart sharpen, then leap, rise closer to the surface of my body. Breathing is one of those things you never notice until it changes.

"Why did you break up with me then?" I try to keep my voice airy, teasing. *I'm not a burden. I'm fun. Someone you want to be with. Someone who makes no demands.*

"I didn't," Adam responds. "If you remember, Natty, it was all your idea."

I can see his mouth, his hair, his eyes. I can see his room, the walls, the rug. His bed, the crumpled bedcovers.

I sigh into the phone. He's going to do this again. I am trapped. Wordless, defenseless, turned around. I am sure this is manipulation. I just can't figure out of what.

Because yes, he's right. In a way. Technically speaking, it was all my idea, but it's not that simple.

If I had to sum up the human condition, I would say life is one big rationalization. Or maybe a series of thousands, every day. Millions over the course of a lifetime. You can convince yourself of just about anything in order to sleep better at night. So if you think you've won an argument, or if you think the reality is so clear and so obvious, think again. When I broke up with Adam for the first time, I never thought he'd agree so easily, so quickly. So willingly. So comfortably.

We were in his room.

Adam had an odd collection of posters on his walls, which by that point I had memorized. There was a poster of Derek Jeter, poked full of thumbtack holes and slightly torn in the upper left corner. Muhammad Ali and Albert Einstein both looked out from across the room. Adam's bar mitzvah sign-in board stood folded behind his door. I had opened it up and read it over and over when he wasn't in the room, trying to absorb any detail, every year and day and moment of Adam's life before me.

I had made it my job to learn everything I could about him. I listened to every story he told. I made observations that would have made my science teacher proud.

Though I doubted Adam could have named my favorite ice-cream flavor, or which AP classes I was taking in school, which CD I've been listening to over and over. Or my birthday.

"This isn't a good relationship for me," I told him.

And then there were the newer decorations in his room. Rap concert posters, ticket stubs, his team photos from lacrosse and basketball. On his desk were his laptop and scattered sweatbands, and one curling picture of me slipped into the frame of his mirror. I had given that to him.

"Why do you say that, baby?" Adam asked me, but his eyes were on his computer screen.

He rarely touched me after we did it. All the urgency gone from him. His body slunk away and slouched in his chair. I could feel his energy collapse into itself, away from me. But he would always kiss me passionately when it was time to say good-bye, as if to distinctly mark the separation.

It was his trademark. The good-bye kiss.

Adam banged at the keyboard. A rapid succession of instant messages chimed in and out, computer buddies opening doors and slamming them shut.

And I was left lonely, but not alone. His smell was

on me, the soreness of my muscles and the memory that lingered between my thighs for hours. The fear that came over me as soon as I left his presence, the fear I had been foolish again. Taken a chance. I read and reread my health notes, and knew that withdrawal is not a viable method of birth control. Neither is the rhythm method. Neither is nothing.

I should have gone on the pill, but I was afraid.

And that's when I told him for the last time. He was self-centered and narcissistic. He paid attention to me only when we were together and couldn't seem to conjure up my face when we were apart. I was taking all the risks. I was the one who left school during *my* classes to be with him during *his* free periods.

He returned my phone calls, but rarely made them.

He took everything I offered, but offered nothing in return.

"My love . . ." Adam responded. "I offer you my love."

Was he kidding?

He was not.

But then for a minute, I stopped. It seemed so honest. So perfect and so true. There is nothing greater than love. Everything else was just material, wasn't it? Or immaterial, depending on how you looked at it. Gifts were just belongings. What did it matter that he didn't buy them?

And after all, I'm supposed to take care of myself, aren't I?

Birth control is ultimately the girl's responsibility. This is the twenty-first century. What am I complaining about?

"I'm completely present," he said. "I am here, aren't I?"

He was. Here. And that was more than I could say about some people. Some people leave and never come back.

No, this is different. He is not good for me. This is not good for me. I have to be strong. I have to leave.

I could feel my heart literally breaking, cracking wide open with familiar wounds and pains I thought I would never feel again. I could feel myself walking away from an offer, an offer I had waited so many years to hear. If you had been walking in the desert thirsty for years and years, why would you turn down a drink of water?

I am here.

You'd turn it down if you knew for sure that it wasn't real. If you knew it was a mirage. Why, then, did it appear to you as an oasis?

I love you, baby.

What is real? And what is not?

What *was* my mother going to tell me just before she took her coat from the hook beside the door, just after she dumped those cookies in the trash? What was she going to tell me?

About love.

"Natty? Are you still there?" Adam's voice on the phone, breaking into the silence (returning me to the Baltimore bus station).

I am standing in the space between a vending machine and the wall. My shoulders are pinned, with my hand holding my cell phone, my hand up to my ear. I can see the grimly lit waiting room, just beyond the half wall. It is filled with people sitting, waiting. They all look pretty miserable.

It smells like urine in this corner. But it is as private as I could get.

Yes, I hear him. An incredible loneliness begins to wash over me, even as we talk it grows stronger.

"Yes, I'm here," I say into the phone.

Then somebody starts shaking the vending machine.

"Ow," I say as my head bangs against the metal side.

"What, baby?" I hear inside the phone. "What is it?"

"Can somebody help me?" It's a little girl's voice. "I lost my money in there. Can somebody help me?"

She is standing in front of the machine, a suitcase in her hand. I watch as she lifts her foot so it is nearly level with the plastic display of candy and kicks as hard as she can. She grunts as she lands her blow, but no candy drops out. She looks like she is going to cry.

She is a little girl and clearly needs help. I can only barely hear Adam asking me what's going on.

I flip shut my phone without saying good-bye and step out of my corner to see what I can do to help.

The second time my mother decided to practice leaving, I was in first grade. It wasn't that what happened was so unusual; it was the look on her face when it was over, like a scientist conducting an experiment, a reviewer watching a movie.

She forgot to pick me up after school.

No big deal. It happens. Even at six years old, I knew that. I had seen it before. I had seen other forgotten kids, whose mothers came rushing in and swooped up their daughters in their arms, smothering them with kisses and apologies.

"I called your mother," the office lady told me for the third time. "I'm sure she'll be here soon."

The office lady, Mrs. Bennett, was nice. She always smiled, and she wore pretty sweaters every day, decorated with a different flower pin. And she was always typing, facing sideways to the front counter, turning her head when she needed to talk to students, smiling when she did, even if she was interrupted a hundred times. I used to wonder if Mrs. Bennett was typing the same thing, day after day, and just never got to finish.

The other two "left-behind" kids had already been picked up—first, Daniel Sou, and about five minutes later, Patrick Murphy went home. My stomach started to growl as the light outside the window went from yellow to orange to deep purple. Mrs. Bennett finished typing.

"Maybe we should call your dad." She smiled at me, searching her files for my emergency cards.

My dad? It sounded serious. You never call the dad unless it's serious. I had only a vague idea where my dad was, anyway. He left in the morning, dressed in a tie, and he came home just after dinner, when my day was over. Sometimes he packed a suitcase for an overnight business trip and left before I even got out of bed. I barely noticed the nights my father traveled and didn't come home.

Call my daddy?

I started to cry.

Mrs. Bennett stood up right away. "No, no, Natty. It's OK." She banged her knee trying to get to my side of the counter. And that's when my mother showed up.

She didn't have an excuse like the other moms. "I couldn't find my keys." "I got mixed up with my car pool," not even "I forgot."

She just walked in the office, her face blank, and said, "Is Natty OK?"

Chapter Seven

Love me when I least deserve it,
because that's when I really need it.
—Swedish proverb

When the girl kicks the vending machine for the second time, the suitcase in her hand comes undone, spilling its contents, mostly makeup, onto the floor—lipsticks and mascara wands threatening to roll away.

"Oh, no," she cries, but she doesn't move. She's young, I notice. Middle school—fourth, maybe fifth grade. I get the distinct feeling she is by herself; the way she doesn't look around for help, knows it's not coming.

"Don't worry," I say, bending down. As soon as I begin gathering her things, she gets down on the floor beside me, as if she were waiting to be told what to do.

I see a loose retainer nestled among her shirts and jeans and underwear, a notebook marked PRIVATE, and a couple of framed photos.

"Are you alone?" I ask her.

She closes the suitcase. I snap the clasp shut and we both stand. She looks at me a minute, and I recognize the face of someone who is searching for a reasonable lie.

"Don't answer that," I say, holding up my hand, and just then, as if my gesture had something to do with it, a loud clap of thunder makes its way from the outside world into the bus terminal. It nearly shakes the room. I notice that the low hum of human voices from the waiting area stops momentarily and then swells even louder in reaction.

"Weather," I say to the girl, as if this means something. I feel like taking her hand.

"Yeah," she says.

"Wanna go check the schedule?"

It's funny because I feel better already; just talking to someone fills up that space, even if it's temporary. We walk together toward the rows of green molded plastic seats in the waiting area. At the end of each row of five, a metal ashtray is attached to the armrest.

"I'm Natalie," I tell her.

She seems to hesitate a moment and then says, "I'm Claire."

The TV monitor in the sitting area tells us that my bus leaves in an hour, at three fifteen, and Claire's not for thirty-five minutes. Without saying so, we take seats together. If someone happened to walk by and wonder, we'd just look like two sisters, two friends, in a bus station.

We could be coming from somewhere, could be going anywhere, and nobody would know one way or the other.

"Well, looks like we have a wait," I say.

"Yeah, we do." She looks at me and kind of smiles.

I can tell this girl is not going to ask me where I'm going, or why, or to see whom. First, because she's too young to pretend to care, but also because she doesn't want me to reciprocate. She won't ask, because she doesn't want to have to tell.

I've heard of people who can identify types of perfume right down to the brand name and country of origin. I've heard of people who can distinguish different regional accents to the exact city and neighborhood and street corner.

Me?

I can feel guilt the way a hound dog can sniff out a bone he buried in the backyard years before.

She happened to be in the bathtub when her sister, Lily, finally died.

Claire slid down against the cold porcelain, and she listened to her mother crying. She watched the water deepen and nearly cover the pale skin of her body, imagining her belly an island, somewhere far, far away. Outside the door, her mother wailed. Claire could hear her father's voice, weak but comforting, thick with tears. He was walking up and down in the hall, in and out of Lily's bedroom.

Lily's bedroom: metal hospital bed, a bureau top completely covered with medicine bottles, paper cups, gauze, tape. And a smell like bitter chemicals and fresh laundry, and disinfectant, and her sickness. Didn't everything smell of Lily's sickness?

But Lily's toys were lonely, Claire thought.

Some had never been taken from their boxes because Lily was too weak to open them. She would die soon, but people still brought her presents when they came. When the visitor left, sometimes her mother would offer the gift to Claire.

"Would you like this doll?"

"No way—that's for babies. I'm not a stupid baby."

And then it was too late to take it back. Claire could tell, by the face her mother made, how she disapproved.

What a horrible and insensitive girl. How could I love this child? How could anyone really love a child like this?

"Lily's at peace now," Claire's father was saying. "It's OK. It's going to be OK now." His voice was headed down the stairs. To call the doctor? The ambulance? A hearse? Is that how they take dead bodies out of the house? But Claire's mother stayed in Lily's room.

Claire wondered how long it would be before someone remembered she was in here. The bathroom door was shut tight. Was it locked? Hot steam still clung to the air. It completely coated the mirror above the sink. Silently, her knees lowered into the water and her feet rose up on either side of the faucet.

A noise came from outside, from Lily's room—a feral, frightening sound, until Claire realized it was only her mother. Claire imagined her mother's body crumpled on the floor, as she had seen her so many times. But her hands, her hands would be up on the bed, holding on to Lily, even though Lily was gone.

Claire wondered what would happen if her mother cried forever, as it seemed she had ever since Lily was born and had started dying right away. Would tears fill the house, flood through the halls, and spill out of the windows until they all floated away?

She heard her father's footsteps running back up the stairs. Clomping. Clomping. Heavy and loud.

"Let her go now. Let her go. It's been so long. So long."

But Claire's mother continued to wail.

Maybe if Claire turned on the water, the pipes would sputter, the boiler would crank on. Water would rush from the faucet and hit the surface, loudly and with urgency. Claire started to lean forward, but instead she stood, completely upright, the water now only covering her ankles and dripping from every surface of her body, her skin wet and beginning to pucker with goose bumps.

Claire turned and looked at herself in the mirror, but she couldn't see anything. It was too foggy, too steamy, as if it was all underwater. She could only make out a shadow of herself in the glass while beads of water formed. While the air slowly cleared.

It would only be a matter of time now. What little heat was left in the room would rise up and disappear. The swirling water would be completely drained. It would be quiet again, except for the noises from outside the door.

She put her hands up to cover her ears. And that's when Claire decided to run away. To see if anyone would notice she was gone. To see if her father would come and try to find her. And convince her she deserved to be alive.

For a second I think that the boy working behind the counter here in Baltimore is the same one from the Stamford bus station back home, like I had come all this way just to end up right where I started.

I am going to buy Claire something to eat, and then I'm going to find someone to help. She is definitely alone, but she hasn't told me that. And she is definitely angry, but she hasn't said that either. If there is some kind of security office here, I've got to find it and let them know.

"Uh, excuse me?" I call out so I can get waited on.

Is that the same kid? It couldn't be, could it? The way this boy's jeans are drooping, his faded T-shirt, and the shape of his hair from the back seem familiar. It's the weirdest feeling, something from the *Twilight Zone*.

Déjà vu.

But when he turns around, I see it is a different person. There is no similarity at all. How weird. Why would I be thinking of that boy, anyway?

I buy one of just about everything they have: little bags of snacks, chocolate bars, and those crackers with the yellow goo cheese you can spread with a tiny red plastic stick. And a bunch of different drinks. It's actually pretty cheap down here. Claire carries the stuff back to our seats while I count out my money and pay.

"Thanks," I say, stuffing my change back into my

bag. I should count it because this guy doesn't look like he can add or subtract, but neither can I, so what's the difference?

I decide what I need is a good sugar rush.

But Claire is eating all the candy. She leaves the pretzels and peanut-butter crackers. She seems to prefer soda over water. It's OK. I bought a lot.

I do notice, though, that she doesn't say thank you. I thought mothers were supposed to teach their kids to say thank you.

"I have a cell phone, if you want to call anyone," I say casually. I hold it out to her.

"I'm fine," Claire answers.

I take the opportunity to check my calls and then I shut it off again. I need to conserve my nationwide accessibility. My reception bars are disappearing one by one.

Claire keeps her suitcase upright between her legs, with her feet like bookends. We can hear the rain outside and the thunder moving away. I am trying to be pleasant; for some reason I feel responsible for this kid I don't even know. But she is not making it easy.

"What grade are you in?" I ask her, figuring school is a safe topic.

She just shrugs her shoulders, her mouth full of Starbursts. You'd think someone this needy and this hungry would be a little friendlier. A little nicer.

Then again, of all people, I should understand how easy it is to be mean. *Easier* in fact.

Leave being kind and selfless to the people who can afford it. To the people who have experienced it for themselves. Do unto others is a very nice saying, but it doesn't really take certain things into account. Basically, how do you know what to do unto others when nobody's done it unto you?

But when Claire goes into the bathroom, I somehow find the Maryland Transit Authority Security Department.

The first thing that changed when my mother took off was dinner. There wasn't any for a while. Just nothing. I was in sixth grade.

I would get home off the bus and my dad would be there already, because, I suppose, he thought he needed to be. Before that time, when my mom was still around, he used to work really late. Now he made sure to be home, but it was in body only. We never talked about what happened. It was almost as if she never existed.

I would watch my dad pour his first drink around four thirty. He always kept one clear-green bottle of Tanqueray gin in the cabinet above the pantry. I'd help myself to a bowl of cereal around five, and another one usually around eight or nine, before I went to bed. In the morning, before I went to school, I'd have another. I liked to vary my choices a little: healthy cereal for breakfast, like Wheaties or Rice Krispies; for dinner, something in between, like Frosted Mini-Wheats or Blueberry Morning. But at night, I'd go all out. The grosser the better, the sweeter the best: Sugar Pops or Frosted Flakes. I even got my dad to buy Cap'n Crunch and Cocoa Puffs, which turns the milk dark filmy brown. My mother never would have bought Cocoa Puffs.

But she wasn't here, was she?

In school, for the rest of that year, I got hot lunch.

One night I heard my dad puking, only at first I didn't know what it was.

I was already sleeping, or nearly. I was still crying myself to sleep pretty much every night at that point, with my face in my pillow and the covers pulled over my head, trapping me inside. But this sound was louder than I was. I sat up in the darkness; I stopped crying and listened. It's easier to listen when there is no light, nothing to distract you. There is nothing but sound, and it was an awful sound.

My heart froze in that moment when you know something is wrong, before you actually register that something has happened. I was afraid before I realized I was hearing something unnatural and scary. In the next second, I knew it was my dad.

Is he hurt? Has he fallen, or is he sick?

I forced myself to get out of bed. The floor was cold under my bare feet. I felt my way along the wall and into the hall, where the noises got louder. For a second, they stopped. It was quiet.

I had never felt quite so alone as in that moment, in the hallway, with all doors closed to me. Darkness behind me, and darkness up ahead. Until the noises started again, abruptly. I pressed open the door to my parents' bedroom and cautiously stepped inside. There was a light under the bathroom door, edging out along the floor in a perfect flat plane. From behind the door, I could hear moaning. My dad was saying something.

Help me. Help me, God. No, no. Oh, God.

And in between his words, the distinct sound of vomiting. I heard the toilet flush, and, too quickly, the door opened. Light instantly filled the room with its severity, and I saw my dad. He was gray, not only his hair, suddenly, but his skin, his mouth, his eyes. Nothing but grayness. He was wearing only his faded boxer shorts and black dress socks. He looked so small and weak. And sad.

"I hate you!" I shouted. "You're disgusting. No wonder Mom left," I said.

I said that, even knowing all the while that it was my fault she left. It was my fault more than it was his. It was like seeing myself, yelling at myself. Only easier.

Shortly after that, my dad started cooking dinner. Chicken potpies and fish sticks, and then later, hamburgers and baked ziti. I never heard him sick again. I never even saw a bottle of alcohol anywhere in our house. Ever.

It all happens pretty quickly. An announcement comes over the loudspeaker and Claire jumps up.

"That's my bus," she says.

"Wait, are you sure?"

"I'm not dumb," she snaps.

"Well, where are you going?" I don't know what else to say. I suppose it's just a matter of time. Maybe I should stall her. Instead, I get up and walk beside her.

I am surprised when she answers me. "To my grandmother's."

I am more surprised by how much I want to believe this.

"She's paying for my ticket." Claire is suddenly talkative. Maybe because she's picked up her suitcase and is walking away from me. "She can't wait to see me."

"That's nice," I say. "Your grandmother must love you very much."

Christ, when did I start sounding like such a phony?

But Claire just snorts. "Love?" she says. "Love sucks."

Then just as she nears the gate, I see the security lady heading toward her, ready to intercept. The woman has a walkie-talkie up to her mouth, and I can only imagine what she is saying. I sit back down, so I can't see Claire's face. I cannot see whether she feels relieved or betrayed, but either way I am sure she knows it was my fault.

I broke up with Adam a total of three times in four months.

Each time it was my idea.

And each time we got back together, well, that was my idea, too.

"You're pretty unforgettable," I said, admitting, I suppose, that I had been trying to forget him. Only couldn't.

"So are you," Adam told me. He sat down first, on the low stone wall in the front of the high school. Here he was waiting, forgiving. Wanting. I had a choice, but I couldn't put words to it, so I couldn't hear it. Instead, I watched Adam as he watched me sit down on the stone wall beside him. An entire length of empty wall and I was free to sit wherever I chose. I looked down, and I sat.

To anyone else it would have been an insignificant calculation—one inch farther to the right or to the left. If I'd sat farther away, or nearer to Adam, he might have read the whole situation differently. And he might not have taken my face in both his hands, pressing his mouth to mine, as he did.

I could feel his warmth through his fingertips and on his lips. I tried to return the message with my whole body, letting it collapse into his presence.

How could I have been so foolish, so selfish? So demanding. The intensity of being apart, the void that it had formed in me, had created a longing for something I hadn't known I wanted so badly.

How many chances did I deserve?

I wouldn't risk it again.

Chapter Eight

Freond, *the Old English word for "friend," was simply the present participle of the verb* freon, *"to love."*

—yourDictionary.com

As soon as I step up into my bus, my eyes are scanning the tops of heads poking over the tops of the tall seats. I am looking for a place to sit. I notice there is a different driver now. Not that I noticed the first one too closely, but this guy is someone new. He doesn't know or care that the last bus driver drove away and left me on the highway. All he wants is my ticket.

"Everyone take a seat," he says. He's already got his hand on that pole lever that pulls the doors shut. The rain is drizzling, cold and steady, seeping under the corrugated awning. Inside the bus, the windshield wipers are thumping back and forth. They are huge, making their way across the entire windshield. It looks like the front window of a spaceship.

"Can everyone take a seat?"

The bus is pretty crowded. It looks like all the window seats are taken. I can sit next to that large skinhead-looking guy picking at his cuticles; a really, really old lady who has that look of smelling like mothballs and menthol ointment; a man with a McDonald's bag on his lap and a hamburger in his hand; or this little, nervous-looking guy with a briefcase.

"Miss?" The driver says this to me directly. "Find a seat already."

Nervous-man smiles at me as I make my way toward him, which I think is nice since he was probably praying for the seat next to him to stay empty, and I am that last passenger to get on and dash his hopes. But he accommodates me anyway, and something about that seems generous, and I think, for some reason, *God, I gotta call my dad.*

What time is it?

I sit down.

I should have called before. My mind speeds through a garbled time line.

I should be up at the ski house with Sarah by now. I should be unpacked and getting ready to go eat dinner with her family. I should be laughing and listening to them telling family stories and family jokes at some restaurant. Sarah's dad always flirts with the waitresses. Sarah's mom always makes us order too much food.

I really should call my dad, but it's another half an hour or so before I do.

It's almost dark now, on the bus and outside. Up and down the rows of seats, people flip on their little overhead reading lights. It's quieter than it was earlier. The guy next to me has his hands folded neatly over his briefcase. I see that he has two rings, one on each hand. Actually, I don't think he's shifted his position once since the bus started moving. His pants are perfectly pressed, and he smells faintly of soap. I think he's probably gay, which is good. He's not paying any attention to me at all, which is also good, since I'm going to have to lie to my dad, right out loud, in public. But I have no choice.

I can probably get away with this.

I flip open my phone. I am always amazed at how much light glows from this thing. The woman in the seat directly across the aisle looks over at me and then quickly back, engrossed in her serious reading. She is in her early twenties I figure. She shuffles her magazine kind of hostilely. She is reading an especially thick issue of *Vogue*. In her bag, on the floor by her feet, I see a stack of four or five other fashion magazines.

I should have thought of that.

* * *

Sarah and I were supposed to meet at the bookstore.

"Hey, I'm so glad you called me up," she said when she saw me. Sarah is always smiling. That is something I had always loved about her. She made me laugh. Telling Sarah something, even the worst, saddest thing, even if I had just been crying about it, always seemed to sound funny. When I told Sarah, I could laugh about it.

It had been that way since second grade, when I first met and fell in love with Sarah. She had that happy gene, and she was willing to share it.

"Me, too," I said. I *was* glad. So glad to see her in fact that I forgot for a moment that I had lied to Sarah, lied by omission but still lied. It wasn't Sarah I wanted to see that afternoon. It was Adam. Only I didn't know if Adam was going to show up, so I needed a more reliable excuse to come into town. I needed Sarah, but I wanted Adam, and I had used Sarah in the worst possible way.

But that's what girls do for each other, isn't it? It's an unspoken rule, right? Love comes first. We are all in this together. We've got to help each other out—sister power and all that.

Sure.

Sarah would have understood if I had told her, so why didn't I just tell her?

This was our favorite bookstore — the only one in town, but still our favorite place to hang. The people who worked there let us read books we never bought, sit on the floor and talk. When we were in fifth grade and too afraid and embarrassed, one of us stood by the window display holding open pages of *Our Bodies, Ourselves* for the other to look at the pictures from out on the sidewalk. Then we switched.

No one in the store ever made us stop.

There were pictures of naked women, people having sex, babies being born. We wanted to know. We asked each other questions we couldn't ask anyone else.

But that day, I felt shame rising up in my face for an entirely different reason. I knew I had betrayed Sarah, only she didn't. Not yet.

"Wanna stay here or go get something to eat? Or see a movie?" Sarah asked me. "Or we could just stay here. Whatever. It's fine with me."

The movie theater was only a few blocks away. The coffee shop next door. I stammered. "I . . . uh . . . um." I moved to shrug, but the weight of my lie, the weight of my truth, held my shoulders down. "I think I'm meeting Adam."

I watched Sarah's face crumble, or drop, rather. All her features that a second ago had been angled up into smiles were now angled down—her eyes, her cheeks, her mouth. She tried to hide what she was feeling, but she couldn't. We used to joke that she'd be a terrible government spy. If the CIA ever came to our high school to recruit her because of her 4.4 GPA, she'd better turn them down.

Sarah was hurt, and I didn't blame her. Everything had changed recently, however subtly. I didn't call her as much, and when we were on the phone, I wouldn't stay on long. I was constantly aware that I might get call waiting and that it might be Adam. I wouldn't want to have to cut Sarah off if she was saying something important. I was thinking of *her* feelings, I told myself. So eventually it just became easier not to be on the phone with her at all.

Sarah and I still ate lunch together every fourth day, when our lunch periods coincided and she didn't have an extra bio lab. (Sarah was one of those girl science geniuses.) But that was only because Adam left school for lunch. He drove in his old vintage colorless car into town and bought pizza. Underclassmen weren't allowed to leave school.

What would he have done if I had been allowed? Would he have taken me with him? With his friends?

Would I have missed class like he did? Come in late for eighth period nearly every single day? Drop a whole grade for every seven tardies?

Oh, yes. Unequivocally. Yes.

"No, I mean, Sarah, I do have a little time. We can go next door and get a mocha cappuccino or something," I tried, but I watched as Sarah went from being really hurt to angry. To something I had never seen before.

"Never mind," she said.

"I mean, I didn't know if he could make it or not. . . . My dad wasn't going to just drop me off in town. I had to tell him something . . . and then you called and I thought . . . maybe. Well, I didn't know if Adam was coming. I just . . . didn't know."

"You called *me,* Natalie. Remember?"

The name *Marissa* is stitched onto her magazine bag, with a large appliqué flower growing out of the last letter. I try to ignore her, although she is practically falling out of her seat to eavesdrop.

I press my speed dial for HOME, and after a long silence in which I can visualize my call as hundreds of molecules speeding around the universe looking for my house, it rings. Once. Twice.

My dad picks up.

"Hello, pumpkin."

He must have finally figured out caller ID.

"Hey, Dad. Can't talk long," I say. I try cupping my mouth and the phone with my hand. I lean my head down toward my lap and hope no sirens race by on the highway, or the bus doesn't beep its horn or anything identifying like that. "Sarah and I have to meet everyone downstairs for dinner in a few minutes."

The woman with her ten-pound *Vogue* is now lifting her head just a tiny bit, keeping her face down, but her eyes shift toward me. I can feel it. I can see her hands tighten on her magazine.

This Marissa woman should really mind her own business, I think.

"It's late. What time did you get up there?" my dad asks.

Shit. It's late? It shouldn't have taken that long to drive to Vermont, four, five hours tops. It's hard to concentrate. Lying takes concentration.

"Well, we ate a late lunch on the road at Friendly's. We all had ice creams, too. So we're eating a late dinner in town. Ron and Debbie are waiting for us in the lobby . . . so I should probably go."

Now the *Vogue* lady is practically gripping a glossy page so hard it wrinkles.

I learned a little bit about lying from my Adam days. I knew my dad wouldn't have liked him being so old. Or wouldn't have liked me spending so much time with him. He surely wouldn't have approved of *how* I was spending my time. So I learned how to throw in a detail or two for authenticity but keep it short. Don't talk too much. The longer you talk, the more likely you are to slip up.

"Whatcha have for dinner?" I ask. I am breaking my own rules.

"Oh, there was that leftover Chinese, remember?"

"Oh, right. That's nice."

I am about to say good-bye when my dad asks me, "So how's the weather up there? Any good snow?"

Now I've done it.

Weather. Weather. Shit. Weather. Can't lie about the weather. It's too easy for someone to check.

It's a funny thing. If I were telling the truth, if I were up in Vermont with Sarah and her family, I wouldn't think twice about getting off the phone, hanging up. Telling my dad I'd talk to him tomorrow. Even being rude. Telling my dad he asked too many questions.

But when you're lying, you feel compelled to be nice.

Parents should always worry when their kids are nice to them. Then, outside, as if on cue, rain suddenly pelts the top of the bus in a nonstop metallic riddling.

"It's great, Dad. The snow is great." Just as I say this, a bright light flashes across the highway and illuminates the raindrops outside like a strobe. They appear to freeze in time, followed by a loud clap of thunder.

"Gotta go, Dad," I say. "Love you."

I flip my phone shut and the magazine lady gives me the dirtiest look, like she's got something to say about all this.

Get a life, why don't you?

Who does she think *she* is? Like she never lied to anyone?

Bet you didn't have any friends in high school, lady.

Seventeen magazine assured Marissa that her prom night would be the best night of her life—if only she were sure to follow seven important steps. *Glamour* magazine had a whole spring issue dedicated to how to look the best at your high-school prom. Have a snack, take a bath, make a list, have some water, strike a pose, advised *Cosmopolitan*. Marissa devoured every magazine article as if starving, hungry for the words that would shape her story. And make her happy.

One magazine suggested getting a tan, so as not to look washed-out in the photos. After all, photos last a lifetime. This was promised to be the best, most important night of her entire life.

Still, as she lay under the lights at Sunsations Tanning Salon for her final twenty-minute treatment before the prom, for some reason Marissa's mind fell backward. And back, so that she couldn't stop it. And it landed her the summer before boys, the summer before sixth grade.

At the Mohonk Mountain resort, where her best friend's father worked maintaining the hundreds of wooden gazebos that sat along the trails, and in the gardens, and beside the lake, in all places of magic. Lying flat as she could, Marissa remembered that she spent almost every night that summer at her best friend's house, and they spent every single day up at Mohonk.

Marissa never took off all of her clothes in the tanning booth, but she lowered the straps of her bikini so she wouldn't have embarrassing white lines. Her prom dress was a strapless A-line, pink. Marissa adjusted the plastic cups over her eyes and settled into the warmth of a coffin that emanated ultraviolet light.

Even though they say you are not supposed to, Marissa felt heat as she fell ever backward.

A single bead of sweat raced down her back, thirst dried her mouth, still Marissa and her best friend wouldn't hide inside, where it was cool. They had to run. It was summer. The whole world was theirs. The entire hotel, the cold glacier lake, the paddleboats, the trails up to the tower, the lemon squeeze, the candy shop, horse stables. Everything but the golf course. You were not allowed on the golf course.

Except of course, late at night, when together they snuck out of their beds. In the moonlight, their white nightgowns glowed like cobwebs after a rain. Freshly cut grass stuck to their bare feet, thick between their toes. No time to stop. They ran. Reaching up into the night sky, pretending to fly, pretending to swim. Pretending, and not having to, because there was nothing but this moment. No need for anyone but each other — to see them, or watch them, or tell them they were content.

They dropped to the damp ground with their arms above their heads, holding each other's hands, and rolled down hill after hill. They stood up, dizzy and laughing, and ran to the next. Never letting go.

Marissa opened her eyes because something gripped her like a panic. She pushed open the lid of the tanning bed just enough to sit up and swing her legs over the side. She didn't even look at the timer. Or worry about her uneven tan lines, or her diet, or the party bus, or whether her date even knew her last name, which she knew he probably didn't.

What was that friend's name?

She couldn't remember. It wasn't that long ago, damn it. What was her name? They had been best friends, the summer before sixth grade, the summer before boys.

Adam wanted me, and I never got a chance to consider whether I had wanted him back or not. Then after a while, that distinction became irrelevant. Because I had fallen in love.

Adam had a way of holding me in his arms that made the whole world disappear. Part of it was his height, that my head rested perfectly in a hidden-away place just under his shoulder. Part of it had to do with the length and strength of his arms, which wrapped completely around *me,* hiding me away.

It was easy to forget about everything else.

"I'm crazy about you, Natty," Adam said.

I liked that, too. Loved it. *I'm crazy about you.* It was better than "I love you." It meant that he was out of control, somehow couldn't help himself. Not responsible for his actions, just as I wasn't.

The first time it hurt.

It did. And I bled a little, like a ritual coloring, rite of passage. I coveted the brownish stain on the inside of my leg, the tiny spots on my underwear. I thrilled at the blood sacrifice. I would soak in every detail, regarding this a milestone. My ultimate passage into womanhood.

Adam drove me home that night; we sat in his car by the curb outside my house saying good-bye. I was still sore between my legs. I had to pee so badly, and I knew it was going to sting when I did. But I wouldn't have shortened this time together for anything in the world, least of all for myself. Our warm breathing, our whispered talking, had already fogged up all the windows. It was mid-October, dark and chilly out. Condensation happens.

Adam wrote my name with his finger on the wet glass. He stopped saying anything. He kissed me, holding my face in his hands. That was his signal. I knew he was ready for me to leave.

Open the door. Get out of the car. Say good-bye.

Sure, I told myself, *I can say good-bye.*

Can't I?

I wanted something in that moment, something more, something much more. A promise of some kind, a long cord. A long invisible cord that would stretch as far as either of us could travel. Good-bye didn't feel adequate at all. In fact, it felt like the antithesis of what I was looking for. There should be some new words for this, another expression. *I belong to you now. I gave myself to you.*

We are parting but only in a physical sense. *I am yours now*.

But what I didn't know then was that just because something belongs to someone doesn't mean they know how to take care of it.

Richmond.

The bus has arrived in Virginia, and it must be dinnertime, because everyone is breaking out the brown bags and Tupperware again. The guy next to me offers me a piece of his sushi, but this time I have some snacks of my own. Everything I bought that Claire didn't like. The woman across from me offers me one of her magazines.

"Thanks."

She's not so bad.

Richmond.

We have a forty-five-minute wait here.

Next stop in four hours. Fayetteville, North Carolina.

Just moving right along.

"Oh, sorry," the man in the seat next to me is saying when his hand slips and touches my arm for an instant. He pulls it farther away than he needs, giving me more than my share of the armrest.

But I appreciate it. He is far too sensitive about my

personal space *not* to be gay, and that makes me feel safe. Saf-er.

"It's OK," I tell him.

"It's crowded," he says.

"Yeah."

He looks at me, and I know I am right. There's just a sense I get from him. Or a lack of one.

Because there is always that radar in my brain that goes on whenever I am near a stranger, someone bigger, stronger. Male. Different. Because there is always a potential danger. Sometimes you can sense it; sometimes you can't. Sometimes it is obvious, and crude, and even illegal, and other times it is not.

Some danger is avoidable; some is not. Some is in our control. Some is not.

In any case, I remember the exact moment I discovered what it was to be female in this world.

To be forever vulnerable.

We were riding bikes, Sarah and I, back to my house from town, our week's library books stuffed in our knapsacks. It was late summer, maybe early fall. I just know it was beautiful out, not too hot. Perfect. Everything was perfect.

Sarah's stick-thin legs, all muscle, stretched out long from her cutoff shorts. I remember my body had gotten rounder, that summer before sixth grade. I had the tiny beginnings of breasts where Sarah had none. The top part of my legs wider than my shins and calves, my hips fuller. It already bothered me; my body embarrassed me. I tried to never let my legs lie flat on a chair or a seat when anyone could see me.

But that afternoon we just pedaled and pedaled, letting our skin moisten with sweat and letting the air rushing by cool us off.

I could forget all those other things, with my body in motion. Free and unseen.

We came to the intersection, where the road split. One way up toward the mountain; the other stayed companion to the river and the cornfields. We both stopped, tipping our bikes with one leg for balance, when a pickup truck pulled up alongside. There was a stop sign, so we didn't think anything of it.

I remember this as my last thought as an innocent little kid: *I am a car. Vroom. Vroom*.

It was the three of us, revving our engines, preparing to pull away from the start with the drop of the imaginary checkered flag.

Vroom. Vroom.

Sarah was right beside me. I turned to smile and wink at her so we could shift our gears and speed off first. She was looking back toward me, but something was wrong. Her expression was locked and blank.

And afraid.

It was a beautiful day.

The sun shining down on the world, my world.

I am a car. Vroom. Vroom.

Then I turned my head immediately back to see what Sarah was seeing. The truck's window was wide open.

The driver was looking back at us. He had one hand on the steering wheel and the other hand in his lap. My eyes were drawn to a movement of his hand, the color of flesh he was holding, the indistinguishable but unmistakable shape. An image imprinted forever on my brain.

Danger. Immediate and primitive, for although I had no reference, it was real. Neither one of us had to understand to know we needed to run.

I flipped my head back to Sarah. Then without a word, and with tears streaming from our eyes, we both turned our bikes around and rode directly into the shelter of the cornfield. When we couldn't ride over the dry mud any longer, we dropped our bikes and ran, as fast as we could. The spiky, broad corn leaves cut at our bare arms, but we kept running until we reached the river.

Nothing happened. Nothing. We waited until the bugs drove us crazy, and we stepped back out to the road. The truck was gone. Our bikes were right where we had left them.

Nothing had happened. But everything had changed.

Sarah's mother forbade her from riding her bike to my house. Too long an empty stretch of road. There were things girls needed to understand. She had been foolish to allow it before.

You rode into the cornfield? She was livid.

I never told my dad.

I wouldn't have known what to say.

CHAPTER NINE

Each time that one loves is the only time one has ever loved.

—Oscar Wilde

People's heads and a bunch of loose belongings suddenly lurch forward.

A water bottle comes rolling under my feet like it's in a big hurry. Then everything jerks back and stops.

The bus is no longer moving.

"Are you all right?" The guy next to me is asking.

"Yeah," I say slowly.

A smattering of overhead lights go on around us, as people wake up and the quiet of the night turns to murmurs and then more panicky voices. The wind still howls outside, and the rain is steady. I turn to look out the window but it is black. All I can see are beads of water and our reflections.

"What happened?" I ask, because this guy is the only grown-up I know here. For some reason, in the dark, this becomes important.

"I don't know yet. I think maybe there's an accident or something. Looks like traffic is completely stopped."

"Shit. You've got to be kidding," I say. I am still groggy. My magazine is no longer on my lap but on the floor by my feet. I must have fallen asleep.

The man murmurs a soft laugh, which I know is for me, for my cursing. "When I was your age . . ." he begins. His voice is almost feminine, calming.

"I know. I know. I'm sorry."

"It's just different now," he says. "By the way, I'm Paul. Paul Brown." He says his name with an odd urgency, like he wants me to believe him. I think he must be much older than I first thought. Maybe my dad's age or even older.

"Hi, Mr. Brown," I say.

"Paul. I prefer it."

"I'm Natalie."

The driver's voice comes abruptly out through the tiny speakers in the roof of the bus. "There seems to be an obstruction in the road. Power lines. I have radioed in for assistance. Please remain seated."

"Shit is right," Paul says, which makes me laugh. I

don't think I've laughed since I left home. What? Ten hours ago? Twelve? I look at the time on my cell phone. Fifteen hours ago. I shut off the power.

"I'm going to lose battery," I say out loud.

"Do you have someone else to call?"

I realize he must have heard me on the phone before, clearly lying to my dad, but he doesn't say anything.

"If you need to, I have a phone." He pats the briefcase that is still on his lap.

"Thanks. I'm fine."

"Kids always say that nowadays, don't they?"

"Say what?"

"I'm fine, instead of no. Or yes. Language is funny like that. It changes."

There doesn't seem to be any particular judgment in Paul's tone. Just interest.

"I never thought of that."

"Oh, yes. Language changes all the time. It reveals so much about a culture. Just to study their words. Names, too. Names change."

Then a red emergency light appears outside beside the bus, spinning around, reflecting off the trees in the darkness, the bus windows, and into the rain again. The police must be here. I sigh, figuring it's going to be a long time.

"Are you in a hurry?" Paul asks me.

I am not in any hurry at all. In fact, I have no reason to believe my mother will be at 1711 Fernando Street when I get there, *if* I get there. I have never heard of St. Augustine, Florida, though it does have a nice sound to it, like a make-believe place.

I have just enough money to pay a cab, find her house, and get a bus ticket back home, hopefully all before spring break is over and I can show up at home without explanation.

"Trying to get somewhere fast?" he adds.

"Yeah," I say. "I guess I am."

Paul Brown nods. "I used to be like that."

Arnie Braunschwiegger loved his English teacher, Mr. Cowell, plain and simple. And he did so from the first moment he saw him, which was the exact moment he knew his love would never be reciprocated.

Not in quite the same way.

Not ever.

Only this understanding did nothing to lessen Arnie's obsession. Once it began, he carried it with him day and night. During the day, it took the form of "arrangements." Arnie drove to school—his father's old Dodge Dart—so he was able to arrive early. Just early enough to pass by the main office, and look casual.

"Has the *New York Times* arrived yet?" Arnie would ask the office ladies. He would be careful to act as if it were the paper he was interested in, its owner only secondary.

But he knew. He already knew, because he had seen the truck outside. Certainly no one else in Harrisonburg, Virginia, got the *New York Times* delivered every weekend. Maybe nobody else in Harrisonburg even read the *New York Times,* to Arnie's knowledge, at least not regularly, as Mr. Cowell did.

"Yes, as a matter of fact," the principal's secretary said. She passed Arnie the heavy paper, tied in twine, across the counter. "Are you going to bring it to Mr. Cowell again, Mr. Braunschwiegger? How nice of you."

She spoke slowly, and the way she said his full name, it was as if she knew his secret. Arnie hated his name in that moment, and he vowed, that morning, that someday he would change it.

"Yes, thank you. I'll take it to his room." Arnie hurried along. She couldn't know. *How could she?*

Mr. Cowell always read the whole paper. It took him the entire week, and by that time a new edition would arrive. If any of his students so desired, they were welcome, encouraged, to join him and read it as well. Mr. Cowell taught them how. He explained all the different sections. There were so many. He showed them how to fold a towel across their laps so the ink wouldn't leave a stain. How to fold the paper and snap it smooth, so you could read without having to take up so much space. And he showed them a whole new world, of "Travel" and "Real Estate." And Arnie's favorite, "Arts and Leisure."

Mr. Cowell arrived at school early each day and thought to bring extra cups of coffee and doughnuts for any student who showed up. But Arnie could never eat in Mr. Cowell's presence. It was as if his hunger vanished, replaced by a new sensation, a kind of joyful agony he came to feel he couldn't live without. In fact, it was almost as if the more Arnie felt his love unrequited, the greater his love grew. The deeper it ran.

The first part of Arnie's arrangement was simply showing up, learning to read the *New York Times,* without appearing too overanxious, too eager. To become as easy and comfortable as the *Times* itself. So Mr. Cowell would look forward to his visits and miss him when he didn't show up.

"Mr. Braunschwiegger, I see you brought the paper."

It was his voice: deep and masculine, but tender, as

if he had really listened and thought about what he was saying in advance. It was also the smell of his cologne, and the way he'd hold his own hands together, rubbing one thumb over the joint of the other, while he was thinking.

"I can always rely on you," Mr. Cowell said. He was behind his desk, grading papers.

Arnie smiled back, but inside, his heart twisted with pain, so much he could hardly enjoy their time together. It was as if every moment simply brought them closer to the end. The bell would ring, and first period would start. He would not see Mr. Cowell again until English, last period of the day. And then there would be other people around. Distractions. It was not as easy to arrange to be seen or even heard by Mr. Cowell. Mr. Cowell might call on another student. He might be standing in the hall, talking in hushed tones to another teacher.

Sometimes, if he was diligent, Arnie could arrange to be leaving school at the same time that Mr. Cowell was heading for his car. And they could talk on their way to the parking lot.

But it was at night, in Arnie's dreams, in the dreams that occurred just before he fell asleep, the ones he still had control over but were magical enough to carry him away, that he could go anywhere he wanted to go. Be with anyone he wanted to be with.

And make them love him, him alone.
I have such an appetite for you.
If only, and forever, in his dreams.

Dreaming, but no sooner do I realize this than I forget what it was I was dreaming about.

I open my eyes, and it is dark.

Where am I?

On a bus?

I'm on a bus?

Why?

A sense of panic that I haven't felt before seizes me in the dark. Not in all these hours. What time is it now? How alone I feel in the dark. Every thump of the bus tires taking me farther away from everything I know to be real, my house, my room, my dad, school, Sarah.

It moves without my permission—and me along with it.

It is the night, I tell myself. Things will look better in the day. Don't listen to your night voice. The night voice is always afraid. It starts to come back to me as I rub my eyes, my forehead, the top of my head. The roadblock was cleared, and the bus had gotten under way. The next few hours are harder to recover in my mind. My legs are aching; my neck hurts.

I look next to me. Paul Brown is sleeping. All over the bus, people are sleeping. I remember: we stopped in North Carolina two hours ago. We waited there how long?

Then how long before we got to South Carolina? Manning, South Carolina? A few more people got off the bus.

What time is it now?

The dream I was having is beginning to seep into my brain, but it disappears again as soon as I try to remember it. I need to check the time, but I don't wear a watch.

I press the power button on my phone; it takes a while to start up. If I've gotten a call *(did I get a call?),* a message, it will beep, even with the ringer silenced. I hold the phone deep in my lap to muffle any sound. It takes forever. Somebody a few rows back sneezes, and then all is quiet again. My cell phone slowly lights up.

1:43.

It is 1:43 in the morning. Sunday morning.

No messages.

I power down and try to wait it out till daylight.

Dreaming.

That I am on a bus, a long silver bus.

Every seat is empty. No one else here. There isn't even a driver, and yet we are moving. I am on my way to school. This is a familiar ride, the rows of tall green vinyl seats. I stand up to see where everyone has gone.

No, this doesn't feel right. I shouldn't be on this bus; everyone got off at school and I forgot to. Nobody told me to. I am missing math class again, and I didn't do my homework. *I've got to get off,* I am thinking. I've got to stop this bus, but there is no one to tell this to. There is no driver, but we are driving. The bus is shaking and plodding along, rocking like a cradle.

I stand up and start to move forward, down the aisle. I have to do something to stop this bus. I have to get to class, but when I look down, I see I am in bare feet. And on further inspection, I see I am in my pajamas.

I am far more panicked about this than I should be, but knowing it doesn't help at all.

I am moving through the night, past it; and night is just about to give way to morning. I wake up to find that my head is resting on Paul Brown's shoulder. *Oh, Jeez.* When I lift my head, my neck is stiff. I bet my face is swollen. My teeth feel sticky. God, I feel like crap.

"Sorry," I try, but Paul is asleep. His head leaning against the window. His mouth slightly open. His hands still clutched around his bag.

I need to go to the bathroom. I get up. My legs feel weak, but they work.

As I walk down the aisle, I see that most everyone is still sleeping. Some people sleep like they are just sitting in a chair and happen to have their eyes closed. Some people look slouched, like they are in bed. They just happen to be sitting up. I feel like I am viewing something I shouldn't be. Some private moments, secret thoughts. There is something oddly personal about this long-distance bus travel. Outside, morning takes over.

Once the sun starts to come up, it seems there is no stopping it. The bus is flooded with the low, streaming light. It shoots its way in across the windows, and I have to cut through the beams as I walk all the way to the back of the bus and into the tiny bathroom. The bulb flickers on when I shut the door behind me. There is a tiny mirror above a tiny metal sink. In the sink there is a small pool of dirty water that quivers with the vibrations of the bus tires thumping over the seams in the highway.

Where are we?

Georgia? Are we in Georgia yet?

It sounds like tapping, rhythmic tapping. A pencil. A heartbeat slowing, about to stop.

I look at myself in the mirror.

God, I do look terrible.

Worse than I feel.

My hair is bunched up, pulled from the top of my

ponytail, and the side of my head is imprinted with two deep sleep lines. I splash some cold water on my face. I rub my teeth with my finger, and I take a piece of gum out of my bag and pop it in my mouth.

And now I start to realize that the bus is almost there. The ride is almost over, and the journey just about to begin.

I look right into the reflection of my face.

What the hell am I doing?

I knew Adam had a girlfriend when we first met. I felt bad when he dumped her for me. I really did. I never met her. She went to a different school; I never had to see her, but I felt bad.

At the same time, it scared me that he had just dumped her, for apparently no other reason. Even if it was for me.

"But why?" I asked Adam one night. "If you say you loved her?" I always dressed quickly, and preferably in the dark.

Adam didn't seem to have the same shyness about his body. He lay across his bed, the sheets rumpled and the comforter lying on the floor. It occurred to me that a lot of beauty has to do with believing it yourself. That half of what we see is just the way it is presented.

Almost like a magic trick, a sleight of hand.

Far from playing any tricks on anyone, I was the magician's apprentice. I helped the magician perform his magic. I didn't really understand it. If I had any power of my own, I didn't know how to use it.

Not like Adam. He had broken her heart. He told her not to call him anymore, yet sometimes she still did, crying on the phone. Sometimes he let me listen to her messages.

"I *did* love her. I still do," Adam said, stretching his arm out toward me.

I was buttoning up my sweater, straightening myself out. I had to leave soon. It was late. I had told my dad I was studying at Sarah's. I stepped farther away, out of reach. I had to go. I had a history test in the morning, and I hadn't even read over my notes.

"I just wanted you more," he told me.

I loved to hear that. *I just wanted you more.* As if having something someone else wanted made it so much more desirable.

But even then, I knew that didn't make sense. If you can love someone one minute and someone else more the next, then chances are there will be another, and another. And nothing will mean much at all. So I looked for deeper meaning. I was desperate to be wrong.

"Well, there must have been something about her," I pressed. "Something you didn't like. Some reason."

Maybe if I could figure it out, I could avoid it for myself. If I asked enough questions, I could learn from history, and conquer it once and for all.

"Let's not talk about this anymore, Natty. C'mon. You know what you mean to me. You know how you feed my heart . . ." Adam paused. He said slowly, "And nourish . . . my body."

I didn't move. Only my brain clicked forward. I was sure Adam had written that to me before, those exact words—*Feed my heart and nourish my body*—in an e-mail. Sitting at my computer one night about a month ago, when it came up on my screen, I thought I would instantly and joyfully perish, evaporate suddenly from complete happiness and fulfillment.

What more could I ever want from life than to hear such words?

And although I didn't perish, if I had, it would have been just fine. I would have died happily, right then and there.

But now, he said it again, slowly as if just considering the words, as if at this moment they had occurred to him. Clearly, he had forgotten that he had written that exact phrase to me just a few weeks ago. Did he think I would believe he was just making it up now? Here? In this room? In the dark, after we had just shared our bodies?

Is that what he wanted me to believe? Did he believe that?

And it made me wonder how many times he had used it before, and not just with me.

They are just words, I told myself. We all use words over and over. It doesn't diminish their meaning.

But I knew better, didn't I?

Somebody is knocking softly on the bathroom door even though I am sure the VACANT sign slides to OCCUPIED when you lock the door.

"Just a minute," I shout.

This bus trip is nearing its end.

I really didn't think this through at all. What am I going to say to my mother?

What if I don't even recognize her?

What if she doesn't know me?

I now realize fully, that the only part of this plan I thought through was how I would tell Adam about it when it was over. I would call him on the phone weeping, describing the trip, the desperation, the explanation.

I would say:

Weren't you so worried about me?

Did you miss me?

Do you understand now?

Do you know me yet?

Please, know me.

In these fantasies, I didn't really consider the part about going through with it, did I? I envisioned the story, but not the actuality. I could hear myself telling the chronicle but not living it.

Does my stupidity know no bounds? I take one last look and chew my gum to maximum teeth-cleaning effect before I spit it out into the slot marked TRASH ONLY. I see my own eyes looking back at me: brown; a little puffy, but clear. I try to pretend I am seeing not myself but some girl, some pathetic girl with messy hair and fabric imprints on the side of her face. And two newly forming red pimples on her chin, not yet ready for popping.

Adam wouldn't want me now, anyway.

Being wanted—when did that become the only thing that matters to me?

My mother sat staring at herself in her dresser mirror.

"Mommy?" I walked in. The carpet felt furry and soft under my feet. The rest of our house had wooden floors. This difference added to the feeling of sanctuary in my parents' bedroom.

She didn't turn around, but I could see in the mirror that she saw me. Was I three or four years old? It was like I had two mommies, one facing me in the glass and one sitting with her back to me.

But there was only one me.

There was no other little girl in the mirror. She was irrelevant. She didn't exist. There was the me I felt. The me that simply was. Another reflection of my mother. Or she of me.

"Mommy?" I said it again.

This time she turned slowly. "My baby," she said. She held out her arms. She stretched out her hands, her long slender fingers, I could count her fingers, press our fingertips together. One. Two. Three. Four. Five.

"I made a picture," I said. It was in my hand, dangling like a surprise, as I climbed up carefully and sat in her lap. I could feel myself in her arms. Her arms were around me; her smell was powdery. Her skin was smooth. I had worked hard on this picture. Choosing the right colors, shapes. Pressing down with my crayons. I hadn't broken one. No mistakes. I had colored it just right.

I felt her shift her legs a bit under me, but I didn't weigh anything extra. I didn't feel gravity pulling me, sliding me. I felt her arms lift me up, closer, readjusting me. We were one form now, one being, one shape reflected in the mirror. This was as it should be.

This felt right.

"I made this for you." I held it up, too close to her face.

"It's wonderful, Natty," she said. But I knew she wasn't looking at it. She didn't take it in her hands, hold it out at a distance, and turn it. She didn't look at it closely, see the colors I had chosen, the way I had filled in the whole page.

She didn't care.

And so the picture I made stopped existing. It didn't matter anymore, stripped of its importance.

I watched my picture flutter to the ground, and I looked up to see my mother's reaction. Her face and my face, side by side. I could see her eyes, boring into her own and then filling with tears.

Now all I wanted was to get away. I squirmed and struggled in her arms. It was over. I wanted to get away.

"You hate it when I cry, don't you, baby?" she said, watching herself in the mirror, as if she were talking not to me but to her own reflection.

She squeezed me even tighter. I could feel each of her fingers pressing into my back. I could feel her grip weaken, and when she lifted her hands to readjust them, I was able to slip out from under her, and run away.

* * *

Florida.

I have to change buses in Jacksonville. I know this, sort of, although I am having that strange, disoriented not-enough-sleep feeling. I need to clear my head.

I am here.

I am in Florida, and when I step outside, I can tell. It's warmer, sunny. I can take my sweatshirt off and tie it around my waist. The air is still and quiet. It's early. Not even seven thirty in the morning. Sunday morning, and I am nearly a thousand miles from home.

No one knows I am here.

"Are you getting another bus, Natalie?"

I turn around. It's Paul Brown, with his briefcase in his hand, stepping away from the gathering passengers. We are all waiting for the driver to take our bags out from the bus storage.

"Yeah, I am. How about you?"

Paul stands just about my height. In the bright sunlight, I see now, he is probably older than my dad.

"I'm staying here in Jacksonville," he tells me. "Are you OK by yourself? Do you know where you're going?"

The driver hauls open the doors to the cavernous underbelly of the bus. The hydraulics hiss as they lift the compartment door. There are suitcases of all kinds, all sizes, for all kinds of runaways. The driver begins heaving them onto the pavement at an amazing speed.

"Sure," I say. I spot my duffel bag on the sidewalk and reach for it.

"I got it," Paul says. He lifts my bag up and down in the air. "Not much in here. You're not staying long?"

"Long enough, I hope."

Paul swings my bag toward me but doesn't let go when I catch it. "Hey, do you need money? Anything? I mean, I'm not being weird. I know it's weird but . . ."

"It's not weird. It's nice. But I'm fine."

"Right." He nods and lets go of my duffel bag. "Fine."

I smile.

An announcement comes over the loudspeakers on the outdoor platform. Due to the delay, the bus to St. Augustine will be leaving in just five minutes.

"That's me," I say.

"Be safe, Natalie. I hope you find what you're looking for," Paul tells me, and then, just because we have been sitting together for the last twelve hours or so, we hug.

He hands me his card:

A. PAUL BROWN, MANAGER
Extended Stay Suites
Jacksonville, Florida

"Glorified desk clerk," Paul says. "But I get to travel a lot. So you can call me if you need to. For anything. Promise?"

I see he has written his phone number on the back, which we both know I will never use. But we also both know it means so much. It means connection. And that's just about all there is in this life, I think. Even the very temporary, even the transient, even the people who you are never going to see again but who exist because we need them to, because we are human.

"Promise," I say. I do.

Chapter Ten

How on earth are you ever going to explain in terms of chemistry and physics so important a biological phenomenon as first love?

—Albert Einstein

St. Augustine, Florida
9:30 a.m.
Current temperature: 61 degrees

There *was* something inside the package that came from my mother.

It could have been an ugly sweater, out of style and too small. Way too small for me to wear, even if it wasn't so hideous and ugly. It could have been a book, a baby book. One that I read five years ago or was the kind of book I would never, ever want to read. It could have been a corny CD, something that the Goth boy, the one with the nose *and* eyebrow piercing, leather pants, and purple hair who worked at Sam Goody told her all teenagers love.

But it wasn't any of those things.

"Whatcha running from?"

I stop. Out of breath. Sweating.

And lost.

I turn to the voice. It belongs to a little boy sitting on top of an old beat-up car. First I notice his southern accent and then the deep, almost blue, dark tone of his skin.

"I'm not running from anything," I say.

"In this neighborhood you are," he says. "Or you should be."

I think this boy couldn't possibly be older than eight, if that. When I look around, I notice I am in a neighborhood, no longer near the St. Augustine bus terminal or a single palm tree. And I am the only white person I see.

"What are *you* doing here?" he says. He sees the same thing apparently, and from his vantage point up there on that car, he's most likely accurate.

"I thought I could walk from the bus station," I say, looking up, as if this were an answer.

"But you were running."

"No, I wasn't."

"You were."

"Well, I'm looking for an address," I say to the kid, although a couple of others have now gathered around him, sliding up next to the car, leaning on it.

"What is it?" one of the other kids says.

Funny you should ask, I think.

"Fernando Street," I say. It is the first time I have said it out loud. "One-seven-one-one Fernando Street."

Another little kid, a little girl, has moved closer, as if I were the main attraction of the morning. "There ain't no street called that," she says almost defiantly. She even juts out her chin. She reminds me of the kind of girl that never likes me, the kind of girl that has an attitude, and I, then, seem to reek of weakness. But at least this girl is younger than me. She's probably five. Six, tops.

"Nah, I know where it is," the boy on top of the car says. He jumps down, and his sneakers slap the pavement. "It ain't far."

I have no idea whether to believe him or not.

"Maybe there's someone else I could ask. A grown-up or something?" I say, looking around. There are a group of men, sitting on chairs outside a convenience store, all smoking cigarettes.

There is a woman walking across the street with her child trailing behind. She is wearing shorts, high heels, and massive hoop earrings. She looks younger than me. She will definitely not like me. And there are two older teenage boys walking down the sidewalk toward us. I notice that several of the houses on this street are boarded up. Two spaces down, a car with no wheels is sitting contentedly on concrete blocks.

"OK," I say, turning back to the boy. "Can you tell me where?"

"Oh, I'll do better than that," he says. "I'll take you."

"Are you sure you know where it is? Fernando Street." I start to spell it.

"He ain't dumb, lady," the girl with the jutting chin says to me.

It is the first time anyone has ever thought of me as a lady, a grown-up. And funny, it should be now, when I am completely lost and pretty much all alone.

But it seems like a good idea to follow this kid. I don't feel like making any more decisions, and I don't feel like getting my ass kicked by a kindergartener.

"OK," I tell him.

"C'mon, then." He is already off and halfway down the street, skipping happily, high above the ground.

The neighborhood changes a little as we walk. I finally get the kid to slow down.

"I'm an old lady," I tell him, and he seems to believe it. "I can't run that fast."

There are a few more people around. There is a

gas station on the corner. A women's clothing store. A CVS. I haven't seen any abandoned buildings in a while.

"Don't you have to tell your mother or something?" I say. We've gone about ten blocks or so.

"My mama's dead."

I am having serious doubts about this kid since he's already told me five or six completely outrageous stories, including one about his cousin Taiesha, who is going out with Jay-Z, and how he himself tried out for *American Idol*. Simon wanted him, but the producers said he was too young. Then Simon and Paula got in a big fight about it.

"Oh, I'm sorry," I say. "About your mother, I mean."

"Don't be," he tells me. "My grandma takes care of me."

"Well, don't you have to tell your grandma then?"

"Nah, she don't care where I am."

Seven or eight out of the ten things he's told me so far have got to be lies; I just hope it's not the one about knowing where we are going.

"Where you live?" he asks me. We pass a post office and what looks like an office building. If he doesn't know where the Fernando Street is, at least he's taken me someplace I can probably get a cab or a bus from.

"I live in Connecticut," I tell him. "You talk a lot, don't you?"

"Yup," he answers. "Keeps the devil away. My grandma says that."

I'm not sure what this means, but we stop walking at the corner and he points. Sure enough the sign that hangs over the intersection and swings in the wind reads FERNANDO STREET. The storefront on the corner is number 1681. 1711 Fernando Street can't be far from here.

"Hey, thanks a lot," I say. "I wish I could give you something."

"Like what?"

"I don't know." I feel that offering him money would be insulting, even though that's probably the thing he'd want most. I know I would. "But you really went out of your way. I mean, can you get back OK?" I add.

The kid spins around on his toes and starts off back down the way we came. "I'm cool," he says. "I don't need nothing."

He certainly doesn't seem to. But I do. I look down the block. There are apartments and flower boxes, garbage pails, plastic garbage bags tied, this morning's newspapers lying on the stoops, waiting to be picked up. I can't see the doors or the numbers, but I know behind one of them is my mother.

Maybe.

I am still not ready.

I turn back down the street the way we came. "Hey!" I shout. I don't know his name. "Hey, kid. You. Hey."

He stops, already a small figure halfway down the block.

I cup my hands and shout, "Wanna get some breakfast? Coffee?"

It takes me a half a second to finish what I am saying, but by the time I do, he's standing next to me, smiling. He smiles like someone who is always smiling. I think he must have the happy gene, like Sarah.

I like that.

"What's your name?" I ask him.

"Tevin."

"I'm Natalie."

"I knew that," he snaps. "I can read minds."

"Yeah, well, so can I," I tell Tevin.

He looks right at me and I look right back.

Tevin's mother was not dead.

She was alive and well, and at home, worrying about him.

Where is that boy? He is always running off.

Tevin was her baby, her youngest of four. He was so quick in every way, mind and body, and Theresa loved him dearly, as a mother loves her last child, maybe differently from the way she loved the others. Maybe more freely. For longer, maybe. Hoping to hold on to something, but more able to let go because she knows she has no choice. Like watching a bird, a baby bird, openmouthed and begging for food in the morning, flying from the nest by the afternoon, landing splat in the grass and stumbling forward, flapping and flapping, and one day flying.

Flying away.

Theresa twisted her hands together, rubbing the skin until she could feel the bones underneath, and it almost hurt. She looked down. Her hands were big. They always had been. There was a time, when Theresa was younger, when her hands embarrassed her. She had worn press-on nails in spectacular colors to make them prettier. But now they reminded her of her own mother's hands, ugly but capable. Not so dainty, but they did the job. Maybe better.

When she couldn't stand worrying anymore, Theresa got up off the couch, walked past the television, and looked out the window. She saw some of those kids Tevin hung out with: TJ and Christopher, and Victor, and that Williams girl. What was her name?

"Hey, Yvonne! TJ! You seen Tevin?" Theresa shouted down to them.

They had funny looks on their faces.

"Where is he?" Theresa yelled. "You tell me, now, y'hear?"

"He walked off with a white girl," Yvonne shouted back.

"What?" Theresa yelled out.

Yvonne just stood there with her hands on her skinny little hips, thinking she was all that. She didn't say another word, and those other boys were being like deaf mutes.

"I'm coming down there. Don't you move, girl," Theresa told them.

That Yvonne Williams didn't know what she was saying. *White girl*. Tevin was probably right there, hiding behind that piece-of-shit car her brother had given them. Still, as Theresa made her way down the stairwell, her heart started beating faster.

What if something *had* happened to Tevin?

Her mouth went instantly dry, and tears stung her eyes with even the possibility. It isn't like she didn't have the thought all the time with her older boys, every time they left the house.

What would she do if something happened to Tevin, although God knows he asked for it—wild boy. Always acting too big for his britches. Theresa felt a sharp pain in her stomach, like she had been punched. Like she was going to vomit. And then, funny, as she tried to take the stairs two at a time, she suddenly had the memory of morning sickness. A wave of nausea that was almost like being hungry but, of course, you couldn't eat. Theresa hadn't been able to eat anything except Cheerios, with no milk, for nearly three months each time she was pregnant.

Damn, where did that boy go?

Theresa was sweating, out of breath. *A white girl? Walked off with a white girl?*

She swore she would never let him out of the house again.

"Nowhere. Never alone," she mumbled to herself, not believing it but swearing on her life. Safe, that's all she wanted him to be, until he ran away again. And again.

Safe, this is what she was thinking as she pressed her wide hands against the two outer glass doors and stepped onto the sidewalk. The air assaulted her in one powerful blast of tropical heat. A warm February, even for Florida.

Those kids were gone. Scattered, of course. They had run.

"Tevin!" Theresa shouted. Her eyes smarted, and then there he was, walking toward her along the sidewalk, like nobody's business.

"What, Ma? I was just having me a free breakfast," Tevin answered. "Whassup?" He moseyed. There was no other word for it. Swaggered, a full 180 degrees with each step.

Theresa smacked him hard, but not too—right across the top of his head. *Smack*. She loved him that much. ~

CHAPTER ELEVEN

Where there is love, there is life.
—Gandhi

I told Adam about my mother just before I left.

I used it. I played it for what I thought it was worth, like a face card in game of rummy, like the string section in an orchestra. It wasn't that I was so desperate. I just wanted him to know me. I thought I deserved that. Especially as he was knowing me in that biblical way.

I used to think that a person would not know who I was, not really know me, until they heard about my mother. Until they knew that I was a girl whose mother had chosen to leave her, who had not wanted her. Whose mother had walked out the door one night and never came back.

Once upon a time, there was a little girl . . .

It was more like a test.

It was late. My dad was sleeping. He didn't even know Adam was over, that we were in my room.

In my bed. Trying hard to be silent.

I told Adam because I wanted to create something that would hold him to me even after he went home. Even when I wasn't in his presence and he wasn't in mine. We could connect in this way, with a shared truth, a story told. A story heard.

"My mom and dad aren't divorced," I told him. "That's not why I live with my dad."

"Hmm?" He rolled toward me.

"My mom. I never see her."

"Why not?"

He was so sweet that night. I guess he had what people call puppy-dog eyes, battened down with long, dark lashes. He liked to look right at me, through me. He'd watch me blush with the attention.

"Why not, Natty?" he went on—listening, I'm sure, more to his own voice than my words.

So at first, I just shrugged. Lingering.

"You are so beautiful," he said, slipping a piece of my hair behind my ear, as if it were his own. "You are. Do you know that?"

If I ever wanted to believe him, it was that night.

"She walked out four years ago," I went on. "I haven't heard from her since."

"She did?"

He was interested. I could tell. It made me interesting. Different. Not every girl has a story like this.

"It hurts me," I told him. "Still. I think about it. I feel like it was my fault. I feel different from other people. Sometimes . . . it takes me. I don't know. It makes things harder. I get mad. Or jealous. Or scared. I miss her."

I was talking but not really hearing myself. I knew what I was saying but I didn't feel anything. It was all true, but it wasn't real.

"So I think that's why I need to know you're . . ." I started. "Here for me, you know? That you're . . ."

It was a mistake. Different is one thing; needy is another. But I couldn't help it. Once I had started, I needed more. I needed something from him that he could never give.

"It's in the past, Natty. You've got to get over it. You've got to be strong," Adam said. He leaned over and kissed me.

"I like a strong woman," he said with his breath against my lips.

Was that what happened to his last girlfriend?

She wasn't *strong* enough? Had I stumbled on the secret and it was too late?

I called Adam on his cell phone just minutes after he left my house that night, imagining his car halfway down the road.

And he couldn't tell me when I'd see him again. He wanted to get off the phone.

"Talk to you soon," he said.

"When?" I asked.

When?

"Lighten up, Natty," he said.

That's when I decided to leave again, for real, for the first time, for the last time, for me. In defiance of, in search of, in need of, something I didn't yet understand.

Now I am standing here on her street.

Tevin ran back home.

I am thinking of that lovesick character in *My Fair Lady* singing that stupid song. Our high school did the play the year before Sarah and I got there. We were still in middle school then, eighth-graders, the oldest in our school, top of the shit-pile, and we went to see the last performance.

In the song, the guy is content simply to stand on the street where the woman he loves is living. Even though she won't give him the time of day, his heart is soaring, his feet lifting off the pavement, seven stories high, just knowing he's on the street where she lives.

"I'll never be like that," Sarah told to me at intermission.

"He's pathetic," I agreed.

"He's hot, though."

"Who? The character? Or the kid playing him?" We had bought two bottles of water and one packet of Skittles at the concession. I passed the bag to Sarah.

She hit me in the arm. "The kid. He's in eleventh grade. It's Nicky Laico. You know, Caroline's older brother."

"Oh, yeah." I took the bag of candy back. "You think he's cute?"

"Yeah."

We would be in high school in a mere three months. I hadn't really thought of it. Nicky Laico would be there, I supposed. Suddenly, I thought of all the kids, and all the boys, that we would be thrown in with next year. Tons of them. Older than us. Sixteen-year-olds. Seventeen-year-olds. Eighteen.

I didn't think Nicky Laico was all that good-looking. How was it that Sarah did?

For the first time in a really, really long time, I thought about "the list," our list. What had happened to it? In retrospect, I was thinking, there may have been some important things on that list.

"Let's make a deal," I said to Sarah just as the lights were dimming for act 2.

"What are you, a game-show host?"

"No, seriously. Let's agree that we will always come first. To each other. That whoever gets a boyfriend, or if either one of us gets a boyfriend, we'll still be best friends first."

Sarah looked at me, the water bottle tipped up to her mouth. "Of course, Natty. Why would you say that? You'll always be my best friend. That comes before anything."

I felt better, but still I had to wonder. This lovesickness seemed to overtake people without warning. Make them do crazy things against their will. Stand on street corners.

I mean, look at that idiot up there singing.

And somebody writes this crap, don't they?

1711.

The number is painted in green across the two glass doors of the apartment.

The apartment buildings here in St. Augustine are different from the ones back home, up north. It's the colors, I guess. Some here are actually baby blue or the color of sand. There are even pink buildings and coral-colored doors. Turquoise balconies, seashell and sand-dollar motifs on the walls and awnings.

Everything reminds me I am not home. None of the buildings are very tall here. They are like the younger siblings, so the sun breaks out over the tops and brightens everything, even the trash that is scattered in the corners and by the curb. I can see why people want to live in Florida. The sunshine is blinding.

But nothing prepares me for seeing her name on the wall beside the doorbell. Even in the deep heat of the sun, I feel cold. I shiver. The only thing propelling me forward at this point is that I am here.

I am here, almost a thousand miles from where I started. Where we both started.

How many miles did she need to travel to forget me?

Did she go a hundred miles but could still see my face?

I watched my mother's focus return to the mirror.

Did she go five hundred and still hear my voice?

Mom, I want the chocolate cookies.

Did she get here, to this town, and stop when all traces were finally behind her? But I was still there. I still existed, even if she couldn't see me. Even if she couldn't remember me. Even if she didn't want to.

I didn't disappear.

It was a pair of earrings.

In the package from my mother. It was a pair of

crystal chandelier earrings, real crystals. Not glass. Beautiful colors, gold and mauve. And just the right size. Not too big and gaudy. Just right. I put them away and never looked at them again.

It was the wrapper. Her tiny handwriting in the upper left corner. Did she put it there on purpose, to tell me something? Or did they insist on it at the post office?

"Uh, ma'am. We need a return address. Don't you want to write your address here?" He hands her a pen.

My mother would have shaken her head, no. No need.

"I'm not saying it will, but your package could get lost."

Lost? Wasted? That did it. She never could tolerate waste.

She takes the pen and hastily writes in her address. 1711 Fernando Street, St. Augustine, Florida 32084.

Chapter Twelve

The heart has its reasons
which reason knows nothing of.
—Blaise Pascal

She doesn't know me, but she figures it out in a matter of seconds, infinitesimal, lingering, endless nanoseconds.

"Natalie?" she says.

I always thought, when I saw my mother, I would look into her face and somehow become healed, sort of in the way those evangelical ministers do on television. Pressing their hands onto the forehead of some blind girl or crippled boy, thrusting them forward almost violently until they collapse, relinquish their will. And suddenly, they can see or walk or hear or speak; all blemishes vanish. All wounds healed.

But it isn't like that at all.

This is real life.

The cars are still driving by, at a slow but steady rate, in the street directly behind me. The earth is still revolving around the sun, at a speed so great, almost sixty-seven thousand miles an hour, that it cannot even be felt. Seven blackbirds sitting on a wire that stretches from the corner of one building to the corner of another suddenly fly away, all at the same time, as if they've spoken together. And just then, from the apartment next door, from one of the upstairs windows, a man in a white wife-beater leans on the sill and blows the smoke of his cigarette out into the world.

All this is real.

When I don't answer my mother, because I can't, her face crumbles into a thousand pieces. I watch it happen, but there isn't anything I can do about it. I should have known.

"Natalie," she says again. This time softer. It isn't a question anymore. It is a dirge.

She is smaller than I remember, and her hair cut short and blunt. For a moment I remember her wearing an elastic headband to keep her long hair off her face while she cooked dinner or did the dishes or gave me a bath. But I don't remember the streaks of gray.

Her eyes are taking me in, and they seem to redden with an immense pressure behind them. But she doesn't cry this time. Instead, she takes a deep breath. "Do you want to come inside?"

This is an interesting question. I am no longer narrating my own story and imagining Adam listening to me tell it. Now I have to take responsibility for the fact that I am here. I have set an event into motion, and I have to follow it through.

"OK," I say.

She hesitates, as if she is unsure whether to turn her back and have me follow or step aside and usher me in. I don't move one way or another. One way or another, and yet I can still let life move me along. I take my first step toward her.

I can still sail as the wind directs, even if it is I who has built the boat and set it out at sea.

Her apartment is on the ground floor. When I rang her bell, I could see her door open inside the foyer of her building. It opened just as far as the chain lock would allow. I presumed that whoever was inside that apartment could see their visitor through the glass and decide whether to ring them in or not. I watched the door close and then immediately open all the way.

It was my mother who came to the door to let me in.

Now I am following her inside. She is wearing a sweat suit, the kind where the top and bottom match.

Gray satin with two black stripes down the legs, like rappers wear. Or old Florida ladies walking the mall. And apparently, my mom.

I wonder for a moment, Did she used to be fashionable? Didn't she once pay attention to what she wore, her hair? Her toenails? I don't remember.

"Are you alone?" she asks me. She looks back toward the glass doors. Is she expecting someone else? My father?

"Yeah," I say.

I am oddly blank. Oddly absent from inhabiting the inside of my own body. I am standing in my mother's apartment, four years since the last time I saw her, and I feel absolutely nothing. All I can do is look around, take it in.

The floor is covered with a large durrie rug, frayed at the edges. There is a beige-colored corduroy couch against the wall, with one of those daisy-yellow and green crocheted blankets crumpled on one end. There is a low coffee table in front of the couch. Maybe she had been just sitting there. A book is lying facedown on the table, beside it a mug and a balled-up tissue.

Suddenly I have this weird memory. Of tissues. My mother always had a tissue in her pocket. Often they'd make their way out and be lying around our house, on the kitchen counter, in the key dish, next to the bathroom sink.

"Dana, do you have to?" my dad would say. "It's really disgusting. Can't you just throw it away after you use it?"

But she never would. Not if she could get three or four or five more nose blows out of it. I never minded, though. She always had one stuffed into the sleeve of her sweater, just in case she needed it. Sometimes they'd fall out and land on the floor. I knew my mother was around when I saw them, a Hansel and Gretel trail I couldn't follow.

Here I am.

I am on a mission, aren't I? I have a job to do. I wonder if my heart is beating so loud she can hear it. Is it beating at all?

"Can I get you anything to eat or drink?" she asks. Then she laughs, a kind of forced, sad laugh. "Not that I have much to offer. I mean, I didn't know . . . I never have too much."

"No, thanks," I say. "I'm not going to stay. I just came to . . ."

I am not ready to finish that sentence. *I came here to ask you something, Mom. I want to know what you were going to say.*

About love.

But what I really want to know is why you left me. How could you do that? How could a mother do that to her child? Was I that unlovable?

"You're not?" she says. "Of course . . . why? I mean, what? Will you sit down a minute?"

There is an air conditioner in the window cranking away. Sheer curtains hang on either side and move in and out, like they are waving to me. I sit down in an upholstered chair. My mother sits on the couch.

It is her face. The same face. If I look too long, my heart will break.

Above the couch is a painting, some kind of abstract oil painting, but it is not framed.

"I just came to ask you something." I say this like I still believe it, like I ever did. The colors of the painting swirl of their own volition.

"You did? How did you get here?" She is holding her own hands, and I remember her fingers. Her skinny bones, the freckles of her skin. Small hands, not like mine.

"Bus."

"Does your father know?"

I shake my head.

Her eyes fill up with tears as the swirling colors in the unframed painting turn faster and faster. The sienna and fire red blending with, yet remaining separate from, the midnight blue and raging violet.

"You really don't want me to cry, do you?" she asks. She is looking right at me.

"No."

"Then I won't," she promises. "I've been working on that."

The last time my mother practiced her leaving on me, she was gone for two whole days. It wasn't until around eight the first night that my dad noticed she was gone. He had come home from work late, as usual.

He said hello to me while I sat doing my homework in front of the TV. He was holding the *New York Times* tucked under his arm, his briefcase in one hand and his car keys in the other. I knew he was already annoyed. The paper had been sitting at the bottom of the driveway since early that morning, and it had drizzled all day long.

I remember thinking, *I should have brought it in when I got home from school*, but usually my mom did that. I had just started sixth grade. It was about a week before she walked out on us for good.

That afternoon when I got off the bus, something compelled me to walk around the house. I don't know why, since I had come home to an empty house before. I had my own key on a long rope, tied inside my backpack just in case, and it had happened at least three or four times. Sometimes my mother was late coming home from shopping or had an appointment. But I was never alone for more than an hour.

The house was spotless. All the beds in the house were made, even mine, which I was sure I had left in a messy heap that morning. The laundry was done, but not put away. It sat at the bottom of the stairs, folded and tucked, like a new baby in a basket.

There wasn't a spoon in the sink. Not a crumb or a water ring on the counter. The dish rack was emptied.

In the living room the pillows were fluffed. The throw blankets set perfectly over the ends of the couch. The toothbrushes in the bathroom were all standing in their holders. The sink wiped clean of any toothpaste. The toilet paper rolls were new.

All this I noticed when I got home.

And then it all began to come together. A week earlier, my mother had hired this guy with his flatbed to come to our house and load up everything she considered garbage. She had gone through my whole closet, draining it of all my clothes that didn't fit, too old, too stained. She gave away all my old baby books, paperbacks, jigsaw puzzles we had done once and were never going to struggle through again.

Spring cleaning, she called it, even though it was fall. It was early September.

Then I notice a casserole in the oven. Not cooked,

thawing. Ready to be heated. And I knew she was not coming home. And it hardly surprised me.

I turned the oven on, 350 degrees.

"Where's Mom?" my dad asked me. He had finished reading his soggy paper.

My stomach growled with hunger, and my math homework blurred on the page in front of me. I shrugged, but I knew, didn't I? I knew, but I didn't want him to know.

"Dinner will be ready soon," I heard myself saying.

I think I was just hoping I could buy some time.

When my mother came back two days later, she apologized to us both over and over and cried and cried on and off for weeks afterward.

Florida.

I accept a cold drink from my mother, and I hold it in my hand, but don't drink it.

"I'm sorry, Natalie," she tells me. "It's almost funny, isn't it? That you are here? I mean, it's been four years."

"Four years, four months, fifteen days . . . sixteen days."

"Four years? Four months?" She says this like the words are rocks in her mouth. "Sixteen days?" When she says it, she looks lighter.

"Yeah, sixteen."

People say that Christmas or Thanksgiving are the hardest times when you've lost someone. I never understood that. At least you are prepared for holidays. You know they're going to suck. It's the moments that blindside you that hurt the most. Like in school, in sixth grade when we got to go into a new kindergarten class and read to one kid. We all got paired up. You met your buddy in their kindergarten room and sat in a cute little corner on a colorful kindergarten rug.

My buddy came toddling over, clutching his favorite book, *Are You My Mother?,* to his chest.

God, I almost couldn't read the damn book, not one word. The sounds just caught in my throat. *Are you my mother? This stupid bird can't find his mother.*

After that, hell, Thanksgiving is a breeze.

"I know how awful it must have been for you," my mother is saying.

No, you don't, I think.

"I'm really sorry." She says it again, and there is something almost brave about it. Like she means it, whether or not I accept it. For once, she is doing something that doesn't depend on my reaction. I can feel it.

It's her problem, not mine. And I don't have to say anything, so I don't.

"I came to ask you something," I say, because I need to focus.

"What? Go ahead." She looks like she is bracing herself, physically. I see her fingers imprinting on the cushion of the couch.

"That day . . ." I am starting. "That night you left . . ."

All she does is nod. Someone must have taught her this. To listen. To say sorry without needing anything in return. Like some kind of dance: a twelve-step two-step. Maybe it's a good thing.

"You were saying something. You were going to tell me something."

"I was?" She looks like she is really thinking, really trying to remember. She is kneading her thumbs, one on top of the other.

"I was so messed up that night, Natty. . . ."

"I know, but you were going to tell me something. You said it was very important."

"I did?" She is leaning a little closer to me. I can smell her now. Her shampoo. The coffee on her breath.

"Yeah . . . don't you remember? You said Nana told you stuff . . . that it was wrong. That you had it all wrong, and you wanted me to know something. . . ."

I hear the rising in my own voice. I am so tired. All of the last twenty-eight hours are flooding back into my mind, the hundreds of stories that never get told, simply because no one is there to hear them. The hundreds more that get locked up inside until you are so angry you forget who you are.

I am so tired; all the faces blend into one and it's funny, when I close my eyes they all look like me. As in a dream, where words are understood but you cannot remember what they are. And feelings are powerful and real, but there are no words to describe them. The kind of dream you would sound crazy retelling but that you feel has all the answers, if only you could just decipher it.

I think of Paul Brown, Claire and Charlene, and Tevin, the little liar that he is. The waitress at Our Dog House, which seems like a million miles away, and a million years ago. I even think of that woman on the bus and this makes me think of Sarah, and I hope it isn't too late.

Sarah.

My dad.

It is all melding together until I can't separate reality from dream, past from the present, want from need. Desire from caring.

And Adam.

Oh, my God, Adam.

I haven't checked my cell phone since Jacksonville. No, not since the bus stopped in Savannah, Georgia. I haven't thought about Adam. Not once for at least five hours, six maybe. Something about that makes me want to laugh. Really laugh. Die laughing.

"What?" My mother is smiling, I guess, because she doesn't know what else to do. "What? What's so funny?"

I can't stop. I am laughing so hard it hurts.

It's true. I laughed too much, Charlene, just like you told me, I laughed too much and I cried.

I am a little girl. I am loved and I am wanted. My mother has her arms around me. There is no other feeling like this in the whole world. I could fall asleep right now and everything would be OK.

This, I can have again, I say to myself.

When I started crying, my mother got up off the couch and came toward me. At first my shoulders tightened and I almost cringed at her touch, but then, after all, it was too much. It was too hard and too easy to just let go. Even though I knew what was behind those floodgates.

They had to open.

She caught it all. I can feel her lips on my hair, on the top of my head whispering to me. "It's OK. Just cry. You can cry. It's OK. I'm here now." I can feel my whole body collapse to the will of another, my mother.

As if in a time machine, I can feel the years going

backward. I can feel spaces inside of me filling up, holes I never knew were there. I could soar.

I can fly.

"Why did you leave?" I am crying. "Why didn't you want me anymore?"

She is petting my hair, petting my wet cheeks, and rocking with my rhythms.

"It wasn't you," she is saying. "It was never you."

But I hardly hear her.

"You never wanted me. I was a mistake. Is that why you left?" Now I am babbling like a baby.

She lifts her face away from mine. "What are you talking about, Natty?"

"I found it. Sarah and I found your marriage license. In the box, on the top shelf of your closet. We found it. I know."

"Know what, Natty? What do you know?"

"I was a mistake. You were pregnant when you married Daddy. Three and a half months. It was all a mistake. That's why you left. You never wanted me."

And I am so sorry. So sorry I've said this. Sorry if it's true. Sorry if it's not. There is no good answer here.

Her reflection in the mirror is gone. There is only me.

"Natty, listen to me." My mother takes my face and pulls it away from her body so she can see me. Still holding it in her hands, she says to me, "That had nothing to do with why I left or what's wrong with me. I wanted you more than anything on this earth. The day you were born, I was born."

I am aware that my nose is running and my eyes must be nearly swollen shut. I get all blotchy and red when I cry. It is not a pretty sight. But you are always beautiful to your mother, aren't you? She is the one person in this world who thinks you are the most beautiful, important person. The most special.

"Then why?"

She is quiet for a while. Gathering thoughts, I now know, she has been thinking about for years.

"I love you, Natty. And I love Daddy. I just didn't love myself," she is saying. "I know what a cliché that is, what an excuse, you must be thinking. What a load of crap, right?" She tries to smile, but her smile doesn't extend completely across her mouth, as if she suddenly thinks better of it. As if she doesn't think she should.

"But my love for you couldn't be all I was. It couldn't be all that got me up in the morning. Even though for a long while, it was. When you were very little, it was more than enough. But when you started to move away from me, to grow up . . . even at five, remember? You were always so full of life, always running off, always wanting to explore."

I am listening. I hear what she is saying, but it doesn't really explain anything.

"I was wrong, Natalie. Terribly wrong, but once I had left, I didn't know how to go back. I didn't know if I should," she is saying. "I thought you were better off with your dad."

Then my mother goes on, "I know what I did hurt you, even though that's the last thing on earth I wanted to do," she says. "You didn't deserve that, Natty."

What a funny phrase. You didn't deserve that.

Deserve.

Perhaps if I were given the power to delete a single word from the English language, this would be the one, along with all those inadequate phrases, and all those misunderstandings and misconceptions. Neither good nor bad.

What do I deserve? What does anyone?

Chapter Thirteen

I hold it true, whate'er befall;
I feel it, when I sorrow most;
'Tis better to have loved and lost
Than never to have loved at all.

—Alfred, Lord Tennyson

We decide to go out for dinner, my mother and I, even though I am beat. I am dead tired. But in Florida you can go to dinner really early and it saves you money.

But first I have to call my dad and tell him where I am. Truthfully.

This is really hard.

I have to call from my mom's house since my cell phone is now completely dead. She leaves the room to give me some privacy. I have all these awful fantasies as I dial the number. He's called the police. The bus company. He's talked to Sarah's parents. The school. My God, he called Adam.

None of which turn out to be true.

"How are you, sweetie?" my dad says. "How's the snow up there?"

"Dad, I've got to tell you something."

So I tell him. Dads really are better than moms in a lot of important ways. They don't overreact, usually. Maybe that's what turned out to be the worse thing for my mom, a guy who didn't have big responses. A guy that pretty much left her to do what she needed to do, as long as it didn't cost him any money. Discretion is the better part of valor, he used to say. Maybe she wanted more than that.

Maybe that was hard for her.

But for me it pays off.

My dad just wants to know I'm OK. How and when I'm getting home.

"Mom says she's going to look into buying me a plane ticket and she says she can take me to the airport here," I tell him.

At dinner, my mother has all the questions, but she asks them slowly, one at a time, like she is savoring the answers or she is afraid there is a quota. I notice she stays away from any subject that might directly involve her, like the house, the garden. Her belongings, her car, which is still sitting in the garage. She doesn't ask about Dad's personal life.

"How's Sarah?" she asks me.

"Well, she's fine."

"But what?" my mother says.

"But nothing. I didn't say anything."

"You didn't have to."

I do miss my mother.

"Well, I haven't been a very good friend," I say.

"Does Sarah feel that way or just you?" She has to put on glasses to read the menu. I don't remember that either.

"Both," I tell her.

"Sarah's a good friend. I bet she's not judging you as harshly as you may think. As you judge yourself . . ." Then suddenly she stops.

She tells me that she works in an office. She's lucky she can walk to work, because she doesn't have a car. She's bought everything in her apartment at tag sales, even her bedsheets.

"Gross," I say.

She laughs.

My mother tells me she goes to a therapist twice a week, but only since she's gotten health insurance at her new job. And she's on medication, but I don't want to hear about that.

Is she happy?

"I think it's a mistake to look for happiness," my mother says. "I think it was my mistake, anyway. I have moments when I am happy. Few. But enough."

I want to ask her if she is ever going to come back. Was she ever going to see me again? How could she sleep at night? How can she look at herself in the mirror knowing what she did?

But I can't.

So I begin again. "You were telling me something that night."

"Yes, you said that. . . . I don't remember."

"I do," I say.

"Tell me."

"You told me you wanted to tell me something." I can hear the water running in the sink. I can see her thin, soapy hands. "Something Nana had told you . . . but you said it was the wrong advice."

I can see the pantry. The package of oatmeal cookies sticking up out of the garbage.

"You wanted me to know something," I say. "About love."

My mother is sitting across the table from me, shaking her head slowly. "I'm so sorry, Natty. I just don't remember that at all. My mother, I mean, Nana, she told me a lot of stupid things."

"Like what?"

"I really don't. I mean, I could make something up. I could tell you a million things about love. But I'm probably the worst person to do that."

Somehow, I am not surprised by this. I have come

all this way, these thousand miles, to find out what my mother was going to tell me. To hear what she was going to say about love so that I could understand it. So I could figure out how to *get* love and how to *be* loved. And how to *give* love, without giving myself away.

And now I know this is never going to happen.

But I also know it wasn't really what I was looking for anyway.

Walking back to my mother's apartment from the restaurant, I catch our reflections in a storefront window. It is a car dealership, and behind the glass sit five or six brand-new cars, shiny and parked at various angles as if they are just moments away from screeching out of the showroom.

I am taller than my mother. When did this happen? It almost takes me another glance to realize it is really me, walking beside this woman.

It *is* me. I have long brown hair that, when I wear it loose and the weather's been rainy or a little humid, curls and separates into long twists. It drives me crazy, but I hear some grown women spend hundreds of dollars to get their hair to do that. My body is tall and thin. The curves and widening thighs that used to make me uncomfortable and self-conscious are part of who I am. I grew into them.

It is me.

And I am not a little girl.

So what has my mother missed? My twelfth birthday? Thirteenth? She was not around to witness them, and yet they took place anyway. My fourteenth? My fifteenth and now what?

No, I didn't deserve this, but then again, who is she to dole out exemptions? Only I can do that. And first, I have to forgive myself for something I had nothing to do with. And second, I have to pay attention to the here and now. Because it goes so fast, and I've got a feeling I've got plenty more mistakes of my own to make.

In her apartment, my mother says she is going to pull out the couch in her living room, but then she realizes she doesn't have any sheets for it.

"Don't worry. I'll sleep on it like this," I say. I pat the top cushion.

"No, no. You take my bed. I can sleep on the couch."

"No." I am firm about this, but still, I am asking. "I want to sleep here. Please. I just need a blanket."

She nods. "I understand," she says.

There is that kind of deep sleep that comes after having stayed awake too long, after having been overloaded by images and feelings and thoughts. The kind of sleep that comes immediately, so that you can't even remember laying your head down on the pillow, or pulling up the covers, or even closing your eyes. This is how I fall asleep that night, to the sound of the air conditioner and nothing more. To the stories I've heard and the stories I've told.

And sometimes, stories were repeated so often, I came to think I remembered them. Like the one about getting robbed while on vacation in Hawaii, on the garden island of Kauai. It was only my parents' first anniversary, but of course, I was there, too, and I was already six months old. They could never prove it, but they later knew it was the overly friendly bellhop. He had brought my parents to their condo, he helped with their bags, he opened the wide doors to the balmy Hawaiian night air, and he left quickly. He must have known how tired they were; they had flown all the way from New York. And there had been a long delay. They hadn't really slept in over twenty-four hours.

Of course—get some rest. Tomorrow morning, you won't believe how beautiful it is here in Hawaii. Breakfast is seven to ten thirty. He held his hand out for the tip.

There were two bedrooms in this condo, but my parents set up the crib right beside their bed, pulled as close as could be, and laid me in it.

My dad took off his clothes immediately, washed up, and went to sleep.

But my mother decided to straighten some things up before she could lie down. She dragged all the suitcases into the other bedroom, which she decided had the bigger closet. She picked up the diaper bag and the scattered toys from the plane trip. And then, just before she got into bed herself, she took my father's messy pile of clothes from the floor, folded them neatly, and laid them on the bed in the other room.

When everything looked as orderly as she could make it she, too, crawled into bed and fell fast asleep.

Our amateur thief didn't venture into the room where we were sleeping, but lucky for him, the bag with all my mother's jewelry and my dad's wallet, still in his pant's pocket, with over a thousand dollars in cash, were neatly laid out in the empty bedroom. He made out like a bandit, which is what he was.

But *you* were safe, my mother would tell me. Thank God, you were right next to us all night. Could you imagine if I had put you in the other room, too? But I loved you too much. I always wanted you near me, she would tell me, every time she told the story.

I loved you so much.

I haven't heard that particular story in years.

I like the rusty sound of the air conditioner. I like the smell of my mother's detergent. I am going home tomorrow. I have been here two days, and two nights. Tomorrow morning I have a flight home. My dad ended up making all the plans. I fly out of Jacksonville and change planes in Atlanta, Georgia, and then fly into White Plains Airport, where my dad will meet me. And the whole trip will take all of four hours and twenty minutes.

For two days I have not turned my cell phone on. It's been charging in an outlet by the couch, but it has stayed off.

So on this, my last night in Florida, I give myself permission.

When I turn the power on, I see I have three new voice mails. They beep persistently. And despite my determination, my heart flips and stammers before I even listen to see who they are from.

Yes, the first one is from Adam.

"Hey, baby doll. I know you like to hear from me. So here it is. . . . Here's my voice . . . my message to you. Na-ta-lie. You know you feed my heart and nourish . . . my body." His voice is almost a whisper on my phone.

Is he serious?

He is.

In spite of this, I press nine to save.

The next message is from my dad.

"Hi, sweetie. It's Dad. Just checking in. I'll be waiting for you at baggage. If you have any problems, just call me. I'll leave my cell on. See you tomorrow, sweetie."

There is a pause and I can hear him breathing, like he doesn't know how to press END, and eventually the message clicks off. I save this one, too.

The last message is from Sarah.

"Hey, punk-ass. Your dad told me where you are. You bitch. Why didn't you tell me? God, Natty. I'm your best friend. I could have helped you, gave you money or something. God, I would have gone with you if you wanted. Well, nothing up here. It's cold as shit. I wish you were here. No, I wish I was down there. Call me. Call me. Call me. I can't believe what you did. Natty, I think it was really great. Fly home safe. Love you. Love you."

Her message is cut off by static. I save it.

I listen to Adam's phone message again. Two times. Funny, all I had to do was not call him for three days and look what happens.

I don't want to make any decisions, but I'm not

going to call Adam back tonight. Not that he asked me to. But I'm not anyway.

Just realizing that I *can* but that I'm *not* makes me feel pretty good. Knowing I could and don't want to, don't need to, makes me feel really good.

Better than I have in a long time.

My last night on my mother's couch. She bought new sheets yesterday, a new blanket and a pillow. For when I come back to visit again, she told me.

I know I will.

Tonight, I don't fall asleep as quickly. I can think a little. I can rest before I fall away. Before tomorrow comes, and I have to leave.

I know there are some things that can be taken from you while you sleep. Some things can be lost, or damaged, and never returned, like jewelry and money.

But there are also some things that are imprinted on your brain, even if you can't remember them. They happen so early they become instinctual, even though they are not. A baby is born knowing how to suckle but not how to kiss. An infant can reach up, as if grabbing for a branch, when startled, but not know how to hug. There is much to learn, like a baby duckling coming out of his egg and connecting to the first moving object he sees. *That is my mother,* the duckling says to himself, and he begins to follow her, copy her, learn from her. She feeds him and protects him, and from her, he learns to hug and kiss. From her, he needs to learn to fly.

From her, he learns about love.

I watch as my mother's shape grows smaller.

They let her ride the little shuttle bus out to the runway with me, although I am clearly old enough to fly on a plane by myself. And now she is heading back. Jacksonville is such a small airport they don't have those long expandable gates. I actually walked outside and up these rickety rolling stairs into the plane. And I can watch the shuttle bus driving away with my mother inside. I can see her waving at the window until she and the bus are as small as toys against the long flat line that is the horizon.

That is one thing I noticed here in Florida. It is really flat, without the never-ending hills and mountains we have at home, and so the sky is bigger. You can see farther around and farther behind you. Maybe that's a good thing.

Me, I want to look ahead.

The captain comes on and tells everyone to shut off all electronic devices. He gives us the estimated time of arrival and even the expected temperature. Then he makes a joke about the cold weather up north. The flight attendant tells us to fasten our seat belts. Seat backs and tray tables in their locked and upright positions.

I am going home.

Nobody is in the seat beside me.

Chapter Fourteen

Love does not consist in gazing at each other but in looking outward together in the same direction.

—Antoine de Saint-Exupéry

I can't believe there's a snowstorm up here. A nor'easter. A blizzard. I can see on the television monitors in the county airport that the news stations have already given it a name. They are already calling this one the Millennium Snowstorm.

But words are important.

I watch the snow build up on the guard railings and parked cars and even the windowpanes. There's a guy out there in one of those riding snowblowers, but it looks useless.

We are lucky our plane landed at all. We circled around up there for a while. I think there was talk of flying back down south a little, landing somewhere else. At least I am here. I am close enough to home. My feet are on the ground.

My dad calls my cell. He can't get through, he tells me. The highway is closed. I can barely hear him. It was a bad connection.

"Don't worry, Dad." I am shouting into my tiny cell phone, as if he can hear me more clearly that way. "I'm here. I'm safe. It's kind of nice here. It can't snow forever."

But I can't hear what he answers.

It is nice here, actually. Compared to all the bus terminals I've seen, this is a four-star hotel. It's small and clean. There's a maintenance guy over there scrubbing the tiniest stains out of the carpet. There is a deli and a huge well-lit bathroom, which also happens to be very clean.

I settle in.

I can put my feet up on the rows of seats beside me, since the airport is fairly empty. I have this book of poems by Emily Dickinson that my mother gave me. She told me to read "This is my letter to the World," on page 211.

I'm sure it's going to be depressing.

And I have my cell phone fully charged.

The snow is falling in black silence, but the bright lights on the building illuminate it in midair. There are already several inches on the ground, gathering higher in corners and curbs, white and gentle. They are predicting two feet by morning.

Airplanes won't be able to land, and cars will be stranded all over the city, power lines will invariably go down, but as the snow falls, it is only serenity that I feel.

I am clutching my phone in my hand, and I think I know a little of what it feels to be a recovering alcoholic or drug addict. Trying not to do something that you know will feel good, so good. Real good, but will ultimately be very bad for you.

I don't want to call Adam, but I am thinking of him constantly, like a really uncomfortable pair of pants that make you look terrible, that you wish you could get home to change out of.

But you can't, so you do the best you can.

I flip open my phone and stare at the unnatural glow of light.

I don't want to call Adam, but I can feel the warmth rise inside my body when I think that it will be his voice to answer and it will be his attention focused on me. Even if it's only for a moment, or an hour. Or another day or two. *Or until I really need something from him.*

I stare at the number keys. I will get a certain high just from pressing the buttons of his number. *I can always hang up if I want to. Just to see if he's home. I can block my number.*

Star-six-seven. The numbers sing a song when I press them.

"Hey, you stuck here, too?"

I look up to see who is talking to me, and at the exact same time I realize I've seen this boy before. But I don't know from where. I flip my phone shut.

"Yeah," I answer. "Are you?"

He is standing, not too close. He doesn't move to take a seat next to me, and I am grateful. I know that wherever I've seen him, it was quick, so what stays with me more isn't his face but a feeling.

A gentleness, and a hope; that's the only way I can describe it.

"Yeah, I got here to pick up my dad, but his plane was delayed in Chicago. I think they'll probably cancel it, but I can't drive anywhere now anyway."

We both turn to look out the window. The snow is coming down at a tremendous rate, it seems a never-ending supply. Not a single car drives past.

"I kind of like it," he says, not really to me. He is looking out the window as if out past the road and the parking garage and the airport itself.

"Wanna sit down?" I say. I move my feet and straighten out my shirt all at the same time. I didn't give it much thought when I left Florida this morning. I am wearing an old worn T-shirt, jeans, and the purple flip-flops my mom bought me.

They look better on you, she told me.

"Thanks." He sits. "What are you reading?" He points to the ridiculously thick book of poems. I must look like a nerd.

"Oh, I'm not. Someone gave it to me."

"She's depressing," he tells me, and for a second I think he is talking about my mother.

"Who?"

He laughs. "Emily Dickinson."

"Oh." I laugh, too, and nod.

"Are you meeting someone?" he asks me.

"Yeah, my dad. My dad is supposed to pick me up. But he can't get here in the snow." This boy's face is so familiar. When he talks, when I hear his voice, I think I almost remember. Then a rush of thoughts and feelings flood my mind. There have been so many faces in these few days, all garbled, and so many stories and connections.

About love?

What about it?

"You don't remember me, do you?" the boy asks me.

"Oh." I am beginning to remember. When he laughs, his eyes narrow into smiling half moons.

"You came to the newsstand where I work. You were there to catch a bus, remember now?"

He is wearing a rope necklace, with a single white

shell that sits directly in that spot, settling against the skin of his neck. And it all comes back to me.

"So how was North Dakota?" he asks me.

"I'm Natalie," I say, and I break into a wide smile, as the world outside sits under a heavy blanket. Unable to move, it waits.

"I'm Ethan. You were going to, but you never did buy anything that day," he says.

"What do you mean?"

"To eat. At the newsstand in Stamford. About four days ago, right? You must be hungry."

"Oh, yeah, very funny. Right, I remember. I'm sorry. Ethan? Wow, this is really wild, isn't it?"

"What?"

"Your being here. Tonight. In this airport. Now, of all nights. And me being here."

"Maybe not," he says.

For some reason, I think I know exactly what he means by that, but I don't say anything. There is no need to hurry.

One man has decided to take a nap on the luggage conveyor belt. A couple crouched in the corner are resting their heads on each other and using their suitcases as stools. The television set is still broadcasting the local weather report, as if it is world news.

"So seriously, can I get you something to eat? Or drink?"

"Sure," I say. "But I think I have to tell you something first."

"Shoot."

"I didn't go North Dakota," I begin. "I never was."

"I knew that," he says.

"You did?"

He nods, still smiling. "You were just messing with me. It's cool."

"Wanna know where I really went?" I say. "It's a crazy story."

I used to think that a person would not know who I was, not really know me, until they heard about my mother. Until they knew that I was a girl whose mother had chosen to leave her, had not wanted her. Whose mother walked out the door one night and never came back.

Once upon a time, there was a little girl . . .

"Will this story take a long time?" Ethan asks me.

"I think it might."

"Then, definitely. Yes, tell me," he says. "I think we have plenty of time. You hungry or something? Do you want a soda, or Snapple?"

"Yeah, I kinda am," I say.

We both get up and start walking together, until we are standing in front of the tall display of cold drinks. And he is reaching for his wallet.

We have plenty of time. I wonder if he is only referring to the snowstorm, like in one of those movies where mountain travelers are trapped in a cabin with lots of time to talk. Or something else.

Ethan lets his hand drop to his side, next to mine. But he doesn't touch me. He isn't like that. He would be slower than that. He is the kind of guy who would ask first. I can tell. We buy two bottles of water and decide to share some cookies.

"So will it be a true story this time?" He turns and looks right at me.

"Definitely," I answer.